Penguin Books
Company for Henry

P. G. Wodehouse was born in Guildford in 1881 and
educated at Dulwich College. After working in London
for the Hong Kong and Shanghai Bank for two years,
he left to earn his living as a journalist and storywriter,
writing the 'By the Way' column in the old *Globe*.
He also contributed a series of school stories to a
magazine for boys, the *Captain*, in one of which Psmith
made his first appearance. Going to America before
the First World War, he sold a serial to the *Saturday
Evening Post* and for the next twenty-five years almost
all his books appeared first in this magazine. He was part
author, and writer of the lyrics, of eighteen musical
comedies including *Kissing Time*; he married in 1914
and in 1955 took American, in addition to his
British, citizenship. He wrote over ninety books and
his work has won world-wide acclaim, being translated
into many languages. *The Times* hailed him as 'a comic
genius recognized in his lifetime as a classic and an old
master of farce'.

P. G. Wodehouse said, 'I believe there are two ways of
writing novels. One is mine, making a sort of musical
comedy without music and ignoring real life altogether;
the other is going right deep down into life and not
caring a damn . . .' He was created a Knight of the
British Empire in the New Year's Honours List in 1975.
In a B.B.C. interview he said that he had no ambitions
left, now that he had been knighted and there was a
waxwork of him in Madame Tussaud's. He died on
St Valentine's Day in 1975 at the age of ninety-three.

P. G. Wodehouse

Company for Henry

Penguin Books

Penguin Books Ltd, Harmondsworth, Middlesex, England
Viking Penguin Inc., 40 West 23rd Street, New York, New York 10010, U.S.A.
Penguin Books Australia Ltd, Ringwood, Victoria, Australia
Penguin Books Canada Limited, 2801 John Street, Markham, Ontario, Canada L3R 1B4
Penguin Books (N.Z.) Ltd, 182–190 Wairau Road, Auckland 10, New Zealand

First published by Herbert Jenkins Ltd 1967
Published in Penguin Books 1980
Reprinted 1983, 1985

Made and printed in Great Britain by
Richard Clay (The Chaucer Press) Ltd,
Bungay, Suffolk
Set in Linotype Times

Chapter One

1

Fork in hand and crouched over the stove in the kitchen of his large and inconvenient house, Ashby Hall in the county of Sussex, Henry Paradene had begun to scramble eggs in a frying pan. His eyes were narrowed, his lips set, his air tense. It needed only a white mask over his face and a few nurses hovering in the background to complete the resemblance to Ben Casey performing a delicate brain operation on television.

In the spacious Regency days of the celebrated Beau Paradene, who had built the Hall towards the end of the eighteenth century, the domestic staff, counting grooms, gardeners, coachmen and kennel maids, had numbered more than fifty, but its present personnel consisted of a single employee, the wife of a neighbouring farmer of the name of Makepeace, and she only arrived at noon. Henry and his niece Jane Martyn, who was spending her summer holiday with him, attended to breakfast.

Just as the gamboge mess was approaching the height of its fever the door opened and Jane entered, a small fair-haired girl who looked like a well-dressed wood nymph. She kissed her uncle on the top of his head and directed a critical eye at the frying pan.

'Too ambitious,' she said discouragingly.

'Eh?'

'Scrambled. You should have played safe with boiled. They'll be lumpy.'

'I like them lumpy. You off?'

'In a minute.'

'You're going to find it warm in London.'

'I expect so. But I'm lunching with Lionel and I want to go and see Algy.'

The Algy to whom she alluded was her brother, a lily of the

field who toiled not neither did he spin but somehow in the mysterious manner peculiar to his kind seemed to get along quite satisfactorily. Henry had once advanced the theory that the ravens fed him. There seemed no other explanation of his continued health and well-being.

'Where's he living now?'

'Down in the suburbs. Mon Repos, Burberry Road, Valley Fields, was where he wrote from.'

'What's he doing there?'

'Nothing I imagine.'

'You're probably right. It's what he's best at. Well, give him my curse.'

'I will.'

'Oh, and get a cook.'

'A what?'

'Cook. Woman who cooks things.'

'What's wrong with Ma Makepeace?'

'Not nearly class enough. For J. Wendell Stickney we must have something much hotter. The best is probably none too good for him.'

It was not often that Jane found her uncle cryptic, for as a rule he was a plain direct man whose *obiter dicta* seldom taxed the intelligence unduly, but this remark, so casually thrown into the conversation, baffled her completely.

'Who on earth is J. Wendell Stickney?'

'Eh?' said Henry, absently stirring eggs.

'Who is he?'

'Who?'

'Stickney, the man of mystery.'

'Oh, Stickney? Exactly what I asked myself when his letter arrived this morning. He's an American and I should imagine pretty rich, for he lives on Park Avenue, New York, which I understand takes a bit of doing if you haven't plenty in the current account.'

'But who is he? And why did he write to you? He must have written about *something*.'

'Oh yes, he did that. Very interesting story. It seems that he's by way of being one of the Paradene clan. He has been work-ing out the family tree, and at some point along the line a female Paradene appears to have married a male Stickney, which makes him a cousin about twenty times removed. He seems to think that we cousins should stick together.'

'I still don't understand about the cook.'

'Perfectly simple. I thought it only civil after he had gone to all that trouble to show that we are linked by ties of blood to ask him to look me up if he was ever over here. So I'm writing him to that effect.'

Jane gasped. She could scarcely believe that even Henry, always a creature of impulse, was contemplating going to these lengths.

'You don't mean you're asking him to *stay*?'

'Of course.'

'Henry, you're *non compos*.'

'What gives you that impression?'

'You know how hard up you are. You can't possibly afford to have house parties.'

'You can't call one American a house party even if he's a very stout American. And as for affording it, I've got to afford it. I'll tell you something, Jane. If Stickney comes and if my luck holds, I may get him to buy this morgue of a house.'

'What! Why would he do that?'

'I must give you his letter to read. It'll show you how steamed up he is about his ancestors. And this is the home of his ancestors. I'm hoping he may feel that Ashby Hall is where he belongs. I'm not saying it's a snip, but it's certainly a good sporting venture and worth investing a bit of money in. Bread upon the waters.'

This struck Jane as reasonable. She ceased to resemble a mother rebuking an idiot child.

'I see what you mean. A sprat to catch a whale.'

'Exactly. If you don't speculate, you can't accumulate. And, by Jove, I was nearly forgetting. When engaging the cook, also enrol the services of a butler, a parlourmaid and a housemaid, and see to it that each is at the top of his or her profession. We mustn't skimp for Stickney. Our aim is to knock his eye out.'

When Jane was able to speak, which was not immediately, she said:

'You can't be serious.'

'Of course I'm serious.'

'But where's the money coming from to pay them?'

'That's all arranged for. I've a little nest egg. I've been putting money aside for months for Duff and Trotter.'

'Who are Duff and Trotter? They sound like an old-fashioned vaudeville team.'

'They sell wines, spirits and liqueurs and have been enjoying my patronage for quite a time now. I was planning to send them a little something on account one of these days, but now they'll have to go on waiting. Every penny must be devoted to impressing Stickney.'

'But suppose he doesn't come?'

'Ah, that will mean that one's plans must undergo a radical change. In that case I shake hands with the butler, kiss the cook, tickle the parlourmaid and the housemaid, and fire them. But what makes you suppose he won't come?'

'He may be one of those terrific tycoons who can't get away from the office for a day because everything would go to pot without their personal eye on things.'

Henry considered this.

'I don't think so,' he said. 'I can't tell you why, but I have an idea he's more the dilettante cultured type. Would a tycoon have the time to work out family trees?'

'Yes, there's that. Wait! Something's beginning to stir. Stickney? Wendell Stickney? I believe we had a thing about him in *Newsweek* not long ago,' said Jane, who worked in the London office of that periodical. 'Keep saying Stickney for a bit.'

'Stickney. Stickney.'

'It's coming.'

'Stickney. Stickney.'

'Don't weaken.'

'Stickney. Stickney. Stick –'

'Yes, I've got it. He has a famous collection of something.'

'What?'

'I can't remember. Pictures?'

'First editions?'

'Old china?'

'Stamps? Lots of people collect stamps.'

Jane shook her head.

'It wasn't any of those, it was something much more exotic and unusual, something nobody would expect. Well, it doesn't matter, does it? If he comes, we'll soon find out. He'll probably talk of nothing else.'

'Tropical fish?'

'What about them?'

'I was thinking that they might be what he goes in for.'

'I doubt it. I'd remember if it was anything like that.'

'Perhaps he takes the collection bag round in church. Or collects fares on a bus. No, hardly that if he lives on Park Avenue, unless of course he sticks to the fares. He could make a nice income that way. Or he may be a man of such striking appearance that he collects crowds when he appears in public.'

It seemed to Jane that it was time the meeting was called to order.

'Henry,' she said, 'collect yourself. This has got to stop before we get softening of the brain.'

'Birds' eggs? Autographs? Cigarette ends?'

'I said Stop.'

'Only trying to be helpful.'

'Well, don't. Any more messages for Algy?'

'No, just the curse.'

'Then I'll be off. Are you really going to eat those eggs?'

'Certainly. Did you think I was going to have them framed?'

'I wouldn't care to do it myself. They look like some little-known Asiatic poison. Goodbye. I'll be back on the three-thirty.'

2

The Mon Repos, Burberry Road, Valley Fields, to which Jane was on her way, was one of the many semi-detached villas in that delectable suburb, and anyone peeping in at the window of its spare bedroom would have seen in the bed, though the hour was approaching eleven, the slumbering form of Jane's brother Algernon.

Algy was long and thin and, however unsettled his affairs might be, always unfailingly cheerful – a quality which endeared him even to those who were called upon to support him. They might deplore his consistent refusal to see eye to eye with the poet Longfellow as regarded the reality and earnestness of life, but none of them had ever denied that he was good company.

Like Abou ben Adhem, he loved his fellow men – with the sole exception of Lionel Green, the ornamental young man to whom in what he considered a mad moment his sister Jane had become engaged – and he was thinking now how particularly fond he was of his old schoolmate Bill Hardy, whose hospitality he had been enjoying for the past few weeks. No question about it, Bill did a guest well, and in due course, when he, Algy, had made the fortune which would surely not be long delayed, he would reap his reward. There was nothing niggardly about Algy Martyn. All that kept him from scattering purses of gold right and left to the deserving was the fact that so far, though full of ideas and schemes, he had not succeeded in obtaining any.

Brisk footsteps sounded outside the door. It opened, and the man of whom he had been thinking appeared.

Nature in her dealings with the human race is given to the playing of practical jokes, and she had exercised her distorted sense of humour in the case of Bill Hardy. A young man of his amiability ought by rights to have had a correspondingly amiable exterior. He should have been round and rosy and beaming. Instead of which, he looked so like something out of a gangster film that a seasoned motion picture director might have been deceived. When you saw Bill for the first time, you did not say to yourself, 'There goes a young man with a heart of gold', you thought of him in terms of sawn-off shotguns and pineapple bombs. It was only when he smiled that you realized how mistaken you had been in supposing that the F.B.I. had him on its list of the Top Ten.

He was smiling now. He smiled a good deal these days, for he had much to be pleased about. A handsome legacy always exercises a bracing effect on a young man, and this piece of good fortune had recently happened to Bill, opening out new vistas to him.

'So you're awake at last,' he said.

'Barely, Bill, barely. But life is beginning to steal back into the limbs. Are you off to the great city?'

'I am.'

'I can't offer to come with you. Lots of heavy thinking to do. My mind is always at its best when I am horizontal. Going to the office?'

'No. Seeing my lawyer.'

'Of course, yes. About the legacy. The mists of sleep have not quite cleared away, and I was forgetting that you had been left a bundle. Papers and things to sign, eh?'

'Quite a few.'

'Don't let the legal bird slip anything over on you.'

'I won't.'

'You have to watch these lawyers like a hawk. Yours is reasonably honest, I hope?'

'He seems to have kept out of prison so far.'

'Good. Excellent. And when do you actually get hold of the stuff?'

'Any day now.'

'And what looks like being the figure?'

'I shall have about eight hundred quid a year.'

'Made any plans?'

'I'm going to get a cottage in the country somewhere and write.'

'H'm.'

'Something wrong about that?'

Algy reflected.

'Nothing actually wrong,' he said. 'But it would be much better if you let me handle your capital and double, if not treble, it in a matter of weeks. I'm bursting with ideas. Take this Valley Fields of yours, for instance. Ever since you very decently gave me a roof over my head I've been giving a lot of thought to life in the suburbs, and one thing that struck me was what I may call its garden fence aspect. Each house has its little garden, and each garden has its fence, and sooner or later the boy in House A is going to meet the girl in House B across it. You agree?'

'It's been known to happen.'

'And what then? He says "Lovely day" and she says "Beautiful". He says he hopes the weather will keep up, and she says, she does, too. So far, so good, but after that problems arise. Each is at a loss as to how to carry on from there, and that is where we come in.'

'We?'

'I am assuming that you will finance the scheme.'

'What scheme would that be?'

'Quite a simple one. We advertise in all the local papers that we are willing for a small fee to give advice in matters of the heart, and we tell the boy how to proceed. We guide his steps and warn him against pitfalls. The girl, too. We put her straight on all her little difficulties. Should a lady shake hands or bow on parting from a gentleman whom she has met only once? Can a gentleman present a lady with a pound of chocolates without committing himself to anything unduly definite? Must Mother always come along? Do you say "Miss Jones – Mr Smith" or "Mr Smith – Miss Jones" when introducing friends? And arising from that, does Mr Smith on such an occasion say "Pleased to meet you" or "Happy, I'm sure"? At half a crown a go we should be pulling the stuff in, and no income tax to pay, for all transactions would be carried through in untraceable postal orders. And we should require for the preliminary disbursements not more than about a hundred quid, if that. Do I see you reaching for your cheque-book and fountain-pen?'

'You don't.'

'I haven't stirred your blood?'

'You haven't.'

Algy sighed.

'This isn't the spirit of enterprise I like to see. What you're short of, my lad, is vision. It's rather ironic that you, totally lacking as I say in vision, should be left all these thousands, while I, who need only a fraction of your bit of cash to lay the foundations of a vast fortune, don't get anything. That's life, I suppose. Well, don't let me keep you, Bill. I'll be thinking hard in your absence, and on your return I am sure to have other schemes to place before you for quadrupling your capital. I once heard of a fellow who used to go up to prosperous-looking blokes in the street and whisper in their ear "I know your secret", rightly taking it for granted that every prosperous-looking bloke has one, whereupon the party of the second part, starting guiltily, gave him of his plenty in order to keep his mouth shut. I believe he cleaned up very substantially. But I suppose the finicky would find objections to that. Smacks a little of blackmail.'

'A little.'

'Yes, discard that one, at any rate for the moment. All right, Bill, push off. When do I expect you back?'

'About six.'

'I shall look forward to it. Close the door quietly and bring me some little present from London. And keep a wary eye on that lawyer of yours. He's probably planning to embezzle your little all.'

3

As the train bore Jane to the metropolis, her thoughts were not on her brother Algy nor upon Lionel Green of the firm of Tarvin and Green, interior decorators and dealers in antique furniture, to whom she was engaged and with whom she would shortly be lunching. Nor, except to try unsuccessfully once more to remember what it was that he collected, did she allow her mind to dwell on J. Wendell Stickney, that mystic hand across the sea. She was meditating on the extremely shaky financial position of her Uncle Henry.

She had always been devoted to him, and this visit had given her a disquieting insight into his affairs. The problem of how he managed to subsist was almost as insoluble as that of how Algy continued to function. Rent from the home farm and one or two other farms would, she supposed, bring him in a certain income, but it was one that called for the most rigid economy, and he seemed incapable of economizing. His, until succeeding to the position of Squire of Ashby Hall, had been a bohemian life, in which being unable to afford things had never been regarded as an obstacle to acquiring them. She viewed the situation with concern and thought what a pity it was that the necessity of earning a living made it impossible for her to be always at his side, seeing to it that he drew the line somewhere.

The train arrived at Victoria, and Jane, pigeon-holing for a moment the problem of Henry and his finances, concentrated her mind, like the sensible and competent girl she was, on the day's schedule. First to the agency in Clarges Street to get that cook and her colleagues. Then to Valley Fields to see Algy. Then back to the centre of things to lunch with Lionel. It was a full programme, but she had prudently made an early start and the morning was still reasonably young when she alighted from the train at Valley Fields and emerged into the sunlit street. And she was looking about her for someone who would direct her to Burberry Road, when she became aware that a few yards from where she stood a certain liveliness was in progress.

Valley Fields is one of those rural suburbs. More lawns are cultivated, more green fly squirted with whale oil solution and more garden rollers borrowed there than anywhere else south of the river Thames. Spreading trees line its thoroughfares, and beneath one of these were standing a boy, a dog and one of those individuals so common in the suburbs, who are sometimes jobbing gardeners but more frequently, like this one, just gentlemen of leisure. The boy was holding the dog on a leash, the gentleman of leisure was chewing gum, and all three seemed greatly interested in something in the upper branches of the tree.

Jane was not one of those girls who when encountering the

sensational pass primly by on the other side, too well bred to give way to vulgar curiosity. She liked to be in on the throbbing swirl of events. She approached the group and asked what was going on, and the gentleman of leisure was prompt with his explanation.

'Cat up tree,' he said, getting the meat of his story into the first paragraph like a good reporter. 'Scared to come down, bein' frightened of the dog. Buzz off,' he added, addressing the boy. 'You and that cheesehound both.'

The boy did so, though with the air of one who would have preferred to linger, and Jane started to take charge and organize. She was fond of cats. At Ashby Hall there were three of them, and her talks with them had always been conducted in an atmosphere of the utmost cordiality. It was plain that the withdrawal of the cheesehound had not had the desired soothing effect on this one's nervous system and that more positive steps would have to be taken. She flashed an ingratiating smile at the gentleman of leisure.

'Why don't you climb up and get her?' she said.

He stared at her amazedly. Her smile left him cold. The suggestion she had made seemed to him the silliest he had ever heard.

'Me?' he said, marvelling. 'You mean me?'

'Yes.'

'Climb this here tree and fetch down that there cat?'

'Yes.'

'Lady,' said the gentleman of leisure, 'do you think I'm an acrobat or something?'

Matters seemed to have reached an impasse, and it was at this moment that Bill Hardy, on his way to the station to catch his train, came briskly down the street and arriving at the tree halted abruptly. It was as if, like Lot's wife, he had been unexpectedly turned into a pillar of salt. Only his eyes remained active. These were fixed on Jane in a look of open admiration, a look that made it obvious that he was feeling that something new and beautiful had come into his life. It was a look which she was not unaccustomed to seeing in the eyes of the men she met, for when, as now, her dress was right and her hat was right and her shoes were right and her stockings were right, she seldom failed to appeal to the male eye, always excepting that of her brother Algernon. Brothers are notoriously stern critics where their sisters are concerned. It was Algy's view, and one that he had voiced fearlessly since their childhood days, that she was a little shrimp. To Bill she had all the earmarks of an angel temporarily on vacation from heaven, and he yearned to do some knightly service for her. In his present state of mind he could have walked straight into the court of King Arthur and taken his place at the Round Table with no questions asked.

'Some trouble?' he said, at last finding speech. 'Can I help?'

Jane eyed him speculatively. Not, she thought, a very prepossessing young man. She seemed to have seen his like many times on the motion picture screen, wearing a Homburg hat and a raincoat and making curt remarks out of the side of the mouth. But she was sensible enough to realize that in a crisis like this the main consideration was not a classic profile. Male beauty is all very well, but it does not help to get cats down from trees. What was required was something tough and of an athletic build, and in this respect the newcomer more than passed muster. He looked precisely the sort of young man designed by nature for the decatting of trees. He might, of course, if he took on the assignment, from force of habit whip out the old equalizer and rub out the cat, but that had to be risked. She explained the situation and there came into his face the look that might have come into that of a Round Table knight when asked by a damsel in distress to cope with a fire-breathing dragon which had been causing her annoyance.

'You want it brought down?'

'Would you mind?'

'I'll attend to it right away.'

'It's frightfully good of you.'

'Not at all. A pleasure.'

The gentleman of leisure found himself unable to share Bill's enthusiasm. He swallowed his gum and unwrapped another piece.

'I wouldn't,' he said, inserting it between his lips and beginning to champ. 'Only go getting that suit of yours dirtied up. What we ought to do is stand under the tree and chirrup,' he added, but Bill had already begun to climb, and so much progress did he make that when a few moments later Jane called to him, he failed to get her message and climbed down again.

'I beg your pardon?'

'I only said Be careful.'

'Oh?'

'Sorry.'

'Not at all,' said Bill.

He resumed his activities. The gentleman of leisure followed him with a pessimistic eye.

'You may well say Be careful,' he said moodily. 'A friend of mine broke two ribs playing this silly sort of game. Fellow named George Turner. Had a job pruning the ellums on a gentleman's place down Chigwell way. Two ribs he broke, besides a number of contusions.'

He was aggrieved to find that Jane was not according to his story the attention which its drama and human interest deserved.

'Two ribs,' he repeated, raising his voice. 'Also cuts, scratches and contusions. I wasn't there meself, but they tell me he comes down like a sack of coals. Eye-witnesses say he bounced three times. What you got to bear in mind is that ellums are treacherous. You think the branches is all right, but lean your weight on them and they come apart. That's an ellum he's climbing now. The proper thing we ought to have done here was to have took a ladder and a blanket and a pole and to have held the blanket spread out and gone up the ladder and prodded at that there cat with the pole, same as they do at fires,' said the gentleman of leisure, casting an unwarrantable slur on the methods of the fire brigade.

Bill was now operating in the topmost branches, and the cat had just come within reach of his groping hand, which she scratched severely in several places. Then, eluding his grasp with a look of cold disdain, she proceeded to descend the tree from branch to branch in a nonchalant manner, a feat which was now obvious that she could have performed whenever she had pleased. Cats, it has been well said, will be cats, and there seems nothing to be done about it.

'It's now that's the dangerous part, miss,' said the gentleman of leisure, turning to Jane with a mournful shake of the head, his demeanour that of a man who has tried to put a brave face on things but feels the uselessness of affecting further optimism. 'The coming down, I mean. I don't say climbing up one of these ellums is safe, not what you'd call safe, but it's when you're coming down that the nasty accidents occur. My friend was coming down when he broke his two ribs and got all them scratches and contusions. George Turner his name was, and he had to have seven stitches in him.'

'Oh!' cried Jane.

'Ah!' said the gentleman of leisure.

He spoke with something of the smug self-satisfaction of the prophet whose predicted disasters come off as per schedule. Half-way down the tree Bill, like Mr Turner, had found proof of the treachery of ellums. He had rested his weight on a branch which looked solid, felt solid and should have been solid, and it had snapped under him. For an instant he seemed about to shoot down like, in the gentleman of leisure's poetic phrase, a sack of coals, but he snatched at another branch and checked his fall. He dropped safely to the ground. The record of George Turner remained a mark for other climbers to challenge.

Jane received him with the warmth his temerity deserved. Then she uttered a cry.

'Your poor hands!'

'It's nothing.'

'Did she scratch you?'

'Once or twice.'

'I'm so sorry.'

'It's nothing, really. I'm all right.'

'That's what *you* think,' said the gentleman of leisure, correcting this view. 'Wouldn't be surprised if you didn't come down with lockjaw from getting dirt in them. I had an uncle got dirt into a cut hand, and three days later we were wearing

18

our blacks for him. Two and a half, really, because he expired towards tea time.'

It was a statement that called for comment, but none was forthcoming, for at this moment from somewhere up the line a whistle sounded and Bill gave a start, brought back from knightly deeds to the harsh realities of life. Speed was required, or he would miss his train.

'Good Lord!' he exclaimed. 'I must rush. Goodbye.'

'Goodbye,' said Jane, 'and –'

But he was gone. Having watched him turn the corner, she addressed the gentleman of leisure, who had begun to speak of the possible necessity for amputation.

'I wonder if you can direct me to Burberry Road?'

He seemed to ponder deeply.

'Burberry Road?'

'Yes.'

'Burberry Road?'

'Yes.'

'Burberry Road, eh? Lady, you're in it.'

'In it?'

'You couldn't be more in it if you tried for a month of Sundays,' said the gentleman of leisure, elaborating his point. 'If Burberry Road's what you want, you've got it.'

'Thank you so much,' said Jane, and a few minutes later she was pressing the front door bell of the semi-detached villa to which a poetic builder had given the name of Mon Repos.

4

Her ring was answered by a soberly dressed man, rather good looking in a seedy way, at whom she gazed in open-mouthed astonishment. He had the appearance of a valet or butler – at any rate a personal attendant of some sort – and how her chronically impecunious brother could be in a position to afford the services of a personal attendant, even a shop-soiled one, was more than she could imagine. It was a mystery as unfathomable as that of how he came to be in possession of a house which, though semi-detached, could certainly not be lived in without at least a moderate expenditure on the part of its occupant. In these stern days you do not get even a Mon Repos for nothing. It has to be paid for in hard cash like the Sans Soucis, the Resthavens, the Wee Holmes and all the other establishments turned out in the same mould by speculative builders.

'Good morning,' she said, overcoming her bewilderment.

'Good morning, miss.'

'Is Mr Martyn in?'

'Yes, miss, but he has not yet risen.'

Jane was shocked. Algy from childhood up had never modelled himself on the poet's lark which was accustomed to be on the wing when morn was at seven and the hillside dew-pearled, but it revolted her to think that he was capable of lying in bed at an hour like this, especially on a summer day with the sun shining and all nature calling to him to spring to life and exult in his youth.

'You mean he isn't *up*?'

The man weighed the question and seemed to feel that her way of putting it, though not as graceful as his, covered the facts.

'No, miss. But I will inform him of your presence. What name shall I say?'

'Tell him it's his sister. Miss Martyn.'

'Very good, miss. If you will step this way.'

And presently Algy appeared in the living room in pyjamas and a dressing gown.

'Hullo, squirt,' he said affably, sinking restfully on to the sofa. 'I was hoping you would look in.' Then, for her eyes had widened in what seemed sudden horror, 'Why are you goggling like a startled fish?'

'Because you present such a ghastly spectacle,' she replied with a sister's frankness. 'Do you know what time it is?'

'I am temporarily not in possession of a watch.'

'Pawned it?'

'It is for the moment in escrow.'

'Well, it's long past eleven, and you aren't dressed.'

'I shall be getting around to it shortly. These things can't be hurried.'

'And you haven't shaved.'

'I'm thinking of growing a beard.'

'Over my dead body.'

'That can probably be arranged. I can't understand the prejudice so many people seem to have against beards. An embellishment of that sort is almost a necessity to a man like me, constantly apt to run into people he owes money to. If I had one, I could dive into it when I saw a creditor coming along and hide inside till he had passed. Walt Whitman used to do it all the time. Cigarette?'

'No thanks.'

'Don't want to stunt your growth any more than it's stunted already, eh? Perhaps you're wise. But you're still goggling,' he said, scanning her closely. 'It's the most extraordinary thing that you, admittedly one of the smallest little pipsqueaks that ever broke biscuit, should have eyes more fitted to a girl of twice your stature. They bulge from their sockets. What's on your mind?'

'I'm trying to decide what you look like.'

'Something the cat brought in?'

'That's right. Yes, that's it. Perhaps the very cat I met when I was coming from the station.'

'I am never at my most spruce in the early morning. You'll see a great difference when I have completed my toilet. I shall flash on the world of Valley Fields like some beautiful butterfly emerging from its crysalis. Girls will draw in their breath sharply and whisper "Who is he?" So you met a cat, did you?'

'Well, not actually, because it was stuck at the top of a tree. A young man climbed up after it.'

'What did he do that for?'

'Because I asked him to.'

'Weakminded sort of bloke,' said Algy judicially, 'risking breaking his ruddy neck to oblige a perfect stranger. Or was he a pal of yours?'

'No, we hadn't been introduced. He just happened to come

along. I said "*Would* you mind?" and he said "Delighted" or words to that effect, and up he went.'

'You wouldn't catch me doing that sort of thing. Remember me climbing that tree when we were kids and the branch broke? It might have been a disaster and, as you are about to say, it was, because I survived.'

'I wouldn't dream of saying anything of the sort. You know I love you dearly. All the same, I'd love you even more if you'd stop just messing about.'

'Messing about, did you say?'

'Well, what do you call it?'

'I call it biding my time, waiting patiently for the big opportunity, holding myself always on the alert so that at any moment its coming will find me prepared. That's the way great fortunes are made. And talking of great fortunes I asked you, if you remember, to ask Henry if he would lend me a fiver. Did he come through?'

'Yes, I've got it. And he told me to tell you that an uncle's curse goes with it. He says why the devil don't you get a job?'

Algy shook his head.

'I can't be bothered with jobs. I'm full of great schemes, and these require my undivided attention. All I need to get them going is working capital. If I had a thousand pounds, there are no heights to which I could not soar. I'd be swanking about in fur coats and Rolls-Royces before you knew what had happened.'

'And where are you going to get a thousand pounds?'

'Ah, that's what everybody's asking.'

'What beats me is how you manage to get along. How is it that I find you in this stately home of England? Don't they charge rent in these parts?'

'I believe a certain nominal sum is supposed to change hands from time to time. Bill looks after all that end of it.'

'Bill?'

'My host. Old schoolmate.'

'Was that Bill who let me in?'

'No, that was the broker's man.'

'What!'

'Acting on behalf of Duff and Trotter, to whom I have owed a trifle for rather longer than they liked. I don't know if you are familiar with these things, but what happens is that they write you a series of letters saying a settlement would oblige, and eventually, when it doesn't oblige, they send in the broker's man.'

'You mean he stays with you?'

'That's right.'

In spite of her disapproval of these irregular goings on Jane's heart was touched.

'My poor lamb! How awful for you.'

'Oh, I don't mind. Nice having him around. Very decent sort, Clarence. His name's Clarence Binstead. He used to be on the stage, but had to give it up because he couldn't combine it with his drinking.'

'So he drinks as well as broker's mans? You're giving me a very sordid glimpse into the lives of the poor.'

'Stark facts of life. But if you were thinking of letting your heart bleed for me, don't bother. He's leaving today. Bill paid him off.'

'That was nice of him.'

'Oh, that's Bill all over. Bighearted. Openhanded.'

'He must be. I'd like to meet him. Where is he?'

'Gone up to London to see his lawyer. About this money he's come into.'

'Has he come into money? Much?'

'Not by my standards. He tells me he'll have about eight hundred pounds a year.'

'I don't call that bad.'

'No, it's something to be going on with, I suppose. And I shall of course give him that fiver of Henry's. Was that a mocking laugh?'

'As mocking as I could make it.'

'All right, stick around and you'll see me doing it. He'll be returning at six or thereabouts.'

'Too late for me. I must be getting back to civilization. I'm lunching with Lionel.'

As she had expected, the mention of the name caused Algy

to snort censoriously. He had never approved of her matrimonial plans and seldom shrank from saying so.

'That pill! I thought he was in America. Didn't you tell me months ago that he'd gone over there to muck up some millionaire's house?'

'He's back.'

'And more of a pill than ever, I'll warrant. I little dreamed that the day would come when my only sister would contemplate marrying an interior decorator.'

'He also sells antique furniture.'

'Makes it worse. I can't follow your mental processes. I can't see what there is in it for you. Surely having to spend a lifetime with L. P. Green is a heavy price to pay for getting your dining room decorated for nothing. You say you are lunching with him. Poison his soup.'

'I don't suppose we'll have soup.'

'Then be on the alert. Have a care that he doesn't get called to the telephone at the end of the meal, leaving you stuck with the bill. Your best policy, of course, would be to sever relations over the after-luncheon coffee. Yes, that's the thing to do. Tell him you've been giving it some thought during his absence, and it's all off.'

'Won't that offend him?'

'On the contrary. He'll applaud your good sense. He knows perfectly well what a hound and Tishbite he is. People have been telling him for years. I was at school with L. P. Green and I have a fund of good stories about him, all stressing his unfitness for human consumption. He has absolutely nothing to recommend him as a biological specimen. I remember once –'

'Goodbye,' said Jane.

She took up her bag and departed. Clarence Binstead, the broker's man, was in the hall, leaning against the umbrella stand. They exchanged civil goodbyes.

Chapter Two

1

It was not without a certain trepidation that Jane went to keep her luncheon appointment. Six months had passed since she had seen Lionel, and picking up the threads can be nervous work after an interval as long as that. She was conscious of a feeling almost of shyness.

Her discomfort was not lessened by the fact that the meal was to take place at Lionel's club, an ancient and sombre institution which he had joined because many of those who belonged to it were men of wealth with country houses liable at any moment to require the services of an interior decorator and dealer in antique furniture. It was only in the last year or so that its conservative committee had reluctantly unbent to the extent of providing a small room where members could entertain their female friends, and it was the last place Jane would have chosen for this reunion. Its atmosphere was one of intensely respectable gloom, the furniture heavy, the windows half hidden by massive drapes and the waiters aged and tottery.

Everything about this club of Lionel's depressed Jane, and not least the ordeal to which visitors were subjected immediately on entering. They found themselves in a vast hall liberally provided with repellent-looking statues and presided over by a porter who might have been the model for any one of them. To him they gave their names and the name of their host, and the porter, plainly not believing their story for a moment but deciding that it would be amusing to lure them on before exposing their pretensions, dispatched a page in quest of the member they asked for, confident that he would return with the information that the gentleman had never heard of them in his life. And that, he seemed to be saying, would teach them not to come here trying to borrow money.

Today the ceremony was rendered mercifully brief. Lionel was standing in the hall, looking at his watch. Seeing her, he came forward to greet her and she was able to perceive that six months in America had done nothing to diminish his spectacular charm.

The authorities in charge of human affairs have decreed, no doubt for some excellent reason, that interior decorators as a class shall look simply terrible. Possibly the thought behind this was that if they were beautiful as well as talented, the mixture would be too rich. There are more hollow chests, receding chins and fungus-like side-whiskers in interior decorating circles than in the ranks of any other profession on the list. Orlo Tarvin, Lionel's partner, for instance, was so definitely subhuman that strong men blinked when they saw him.

But every now and then a few can be found who deviate from this norm, and prominent among these was the L. P. Green whom Algy disliked so much. With his melting hazel eyes, his perfectly modelled features, his silky moustache and his flashing smile he might have been a motion picture star whose face had launched a thousand bags of popcorn.

The flashing smile was not at the moment in evidence. He seemed preoccupied, even embarrassed.

'Oh, there you are,' he said, and Jane, already discouraged by the porter, felt additionally damped by the absence from his manner of the fervent and impassioned. It was not thus that she had expected to be greeted after their six months parting. Then she reminded herself that he could hardly have been effusive with the porter's eye upon him. Complaints would have been made to the committee.

'Hullo, Lionel,' she said. 'I'm not late, am I?'

'A few minutes.'

'Sorry. I had to go all the way down to Valley Fields to see Algy.'

'Oh?' said Lionel, plainly revolted that she should have been moving in such company. The want of affection between him and Algy had always been mutual.

'He's living there with a friend of his.'

'Oh?'

'I came away as soon as I could.'

'Quite. I'm glad you're on time,' said Lionel, 'because I've asked a man to join us.'

Jane stared. She thought she must have heard him incorrectly.

'You've ... *what*?'

'My partner, Orlo Tarvin. You'll like him.'

'Oh, shall I?'

'I'm sure you will. Most interesting man. Ah, there he is,' said Lionel, and Jane observed a weird little weedy object approaching. It was wearing harlequin glasses, an Ascot tie, the customary side-whiskers and a beard. The beard was not a large one – Walt Whitman could not have hidden inside it – but it was large enough to send a quick shudder running through her. The thought occurred to her that Lionel probably enjoyed his partner's company because the contrast between them heightened his own comeliness, just as a beautiful girl likes to take a plain friend about with her.

She came out of a momentary coma to find that Orlo Tarvin had possessed himself of both her hands and was gazing meltingly at her.

'My dear!' he was saying. 'I couldn't be more delighted. Lionel has told me so much about you. Don't you think he is looking terribly well after his trip to America? He must tell you all about it at lunch.'

'Yes, let's go in,' said Lionel.

As they made their way to the oubliette to which feminine guests of the club were confined, Jane was aware of an odd and disagreeable feeling. Analysing this, she found that what was causing it was what Roget in his Thesaurus would have called violent anger, extreme agitation, fury, wrath and the rest of the emotions listed under the heading of 'Rage'. As she thought of how Lionel, after a six months parting, had turned the tête-à-tête to which she had been looking forward into a threesome that included the bearded Tarvin, fume, frenzy and *acharnement* bubbled and sizzled within her as if they had been the scrambled eggs assembled in his frying pan that morning by her Uncle Henry.

2

The afternoon wore on. Jane lunched with Lionel Green and his friend Orlo Tarvin. Bill Hardy lunched with his lawyer. Algy, still in pyjamas and dressing gown, lunched off sardines and bottled beer at Mon Repos. Clarence Binstead presumably lunched somewhere. At 3.30 Jane caught the fast train to Ashby Paradene. And at five o'clock Henry Paradene sat in a deck chair on the lawn at Ashby Hall, trying to rough out his letter of invitation to J. Wendell Stickney. His eyes were closed, the better to assist thought. He was finding composition difficult.

Opening his eyes, he took up his task again, but once more inspiration failed. He had never been a ready letter writer. He rose from his chair and began to pace the lawn – an injudicious move, for by doing so he could not fail to see Ashby Hall, a spectacle always calculated to lower his spirits. He sometimes wondered what crime he could inadvertently have committed that had called for the penalty of having that curious edifice inflicted on him.

Some men are born to country houses, some achieve country houses, others have country houses thrust upon them. It was to this last section that Henry belonged. Until succeeding to what was left of the family possessions he had made his living on the musical comedy stage, and it was only owing to the deaths of a number of relatives of whose existence he had been barely aware that he had become the squire of Ashby Hall, where there had been Paradenes for more than four hundred years.

It was a position which at one time would have been considered enviable, but this happy state of things no longer prevailed. Ashby Hall was not the place it had been. Today it had a seedy look. It needed money spent on it, and of money in the Paradene family there had been for several generations an unfortunate lack.

This was due to the activities of the Beau Paradene of whom mention was made earlier. A practical man, he had felt that as you could not take it with you, the shrewd thing to do was to spend it while you had it, and it was a dull night at Watier's or the Cocoa Tree when he was not at the gaming tables losing his thousands of guineas. He had also incurred a great deal of expense by burning the original Elizabethan house to ashes one night when in his cups and causing to be erected in its place a hideous pile that looked partly like the Prince Regent's establishment at Brighton and partly like a mediaeval fortress. Local humourists were accustomed to speak derisively of it as The Castle. Henry himself disliked the place extremely and often thought nostalgically of theatrical lodgings in Middlesbrough and Huddersfield.

For some moments he stood gazing bleakly at the unpleasant structure: then, feeling philosophically that this would do nothing to change it for the better, he resumed his seat and began to write.

'Dear Mr Stickney.'

Extraordinary how difficult it was to get past that promising opening sentence. If only he had known what it was that this distant relative of his collected, he felt, it would all have been simple. How are the first editions coming along, he could have said. Have you bought any good stamps lately? Or Dear Mr Stickney, how I wish I could see those tropical fish of yours. But these avenues were closed to him. All he could do was chew the end of his fountain-pen, never a very satisfactory procedure, for the unyielding nature of the fountain-pen makes it poor chewing.

He was still pondering and no nearer to finding a solution to his problems, when a shadow fell on the page and glancing up he saw his niece Jane.

She eyed him with affectionate approval, thinking, as always when they met, how handsome and distinguished he looked. Henry was now in his fifties but still as slender as in the days when he had done his three dances nightly and at matinées with the soubrette. It had always been the soubrette, for he had never risen higher than second juvenile. Not that this had in the least soured his amiable and easygoing nature. Give him health and his salary on Friday night, and he asked no more.

'Hullo, young Jane,' he said. 'I nearly came to meet you at the station, but I had this damned Stickney letter to write. Did you get the cook?'

'I did.'

'And the rest of the staff?'

'Down to the last housemaid.'

'Good girl. A great organizer, our Jane. Did you see Algy?'

'I saw him, and a horrible sight he was.'

'How's he getting along?'

'Splendidly, as far as I could see. Not a care in the world. He's living with a friend of his called Bill. Bill pays the bills. I gave him the fiver.'

'With my curse?'

'Yes, I remembered to do that.'

'I wish that boy would get a job.'

'So I told him, but he said he hasn't time. Too busy thinking out great schemes.'

'Blister his insides. I'm very fond of Algy, but I repeat – Blister his insides. The maddening thing about him is that one of these days he really may pull something off and make his fortune, and then we shall all look pretty silly. You never know with the Algies of this world. He reminds me of a fellow in a book I was reading who put every penny he had or could borrow into rubber. His friends tried to reason with him. Did he know anything about rubber? Yes, he'd once bought a little square of it when he was a boy, to take out pencil marks. Had he studied the rubber market. He didn't think there was a special rubber market, he'd got his little square at the stationer's. So he put in all this money, and came out a week later with a profit of five thousand pounds. That's Algy. Amazing chap. I suppose you had some difficulty in preventing him coming to join your lunch party?'

'No, he didn't offer to do that.'

'You surprise me. A free meal, and he made no attempt to include himself in? How did it go off?'

Jane winced.

'Not too well.'

'What went wrong?'

'I'll tell you what went wrong,' cried Jane, glad of the opportunity to ease the stuffed bosom of the perilous stuff that weighs upon the heart. There was no one to whom she would have been readier to pour out her troubles than Henry. 'You'll never believe this. You know how long it is since I saw Lionel.'

'Six months, isn't it?'

'About that. Well, I got to his foul ghastly club, all eagerness for the cosy lunch and the cosy talk, just the two of us, and the first thing he tells me is that he has asked a friend of his to join us.'

'What!'

'Yes. His partner, a Mr Tarvin.'

'You're pulling my leg.'

'No, that's what happened.'

'But what an extraordinary thing to do.'

'It did strike me as rather odd. And he seemed all different somehow.'

'In what way?' said Henry, feeling privately that any change in Lionel Green would be for the better.

'Sort of embarrassed. Ill at ease, if you know what I mean. He hardly uttered a word. But let's talk of something else. The cook arrives tomorrow, the rest of the multitude in a day or two.'

'What's the cook like?'

'Long on references, but short on personal charm. I doubt if she gets whistled at much when she takes her walks abroad. Which book of Dickens's is it where there's a woman who looked like Hamlet's aunt? That's Mrs Simmons. On the sombre side.'

'Well, we don't want a lively and vivacious cook.'

'We shan't want any sort of cook if your man Stickney doesn't materialize. Have you finished your letter to him?'

'Not quite.'

'How far have you got?'

' "Dear Mr Stickney".'

'Well, that's a start, and by no means a bad one. I'll help you with the rest of it.'

3

On Jane's departure Algy had continued to pass a pleasant and restful day. At six o'clock, when Bill Hardy returned, he was reclining once more on the living room sofa. He did not rise to greet him, but went so far as to raise a languid hand in welcome.

'Ah, Bill,' he said. 'So you're back. You've just missed my sister. Well, when I say "just", by about seven hours. She left around half past eleven.'

'I didn't know you had a sister.'

'Had her for years. Well, what's your news? How was your lawyer?'

'About the same as ever, except that this time he gave me lunch.'

Algy shook his head.

'I don't like the sound of that. One gets the feeling that he's softening you up preparatory to making a touch. Don't give him a penny. Stick to your money like glue. Oh, and by the way add this to it.'

'What's that?'

'A Treasury note for five, donated by an uncle of mine.'

'I don't want it.'

'You're going to get it. I owe it to my self-respect to do my bit towards the household expenses.'

'Well, all right,' said Bill reluctantly. 'If that's how you feel.'

He stretched out a hand, and Algy cocked an inquiring eye at it.

'Hullo!' he said.

'Those scratches?' said Bill. 'I got those –'

Algy held up a restraining hand.

'No need to tell me. I was afraid something like this would happen one of these days. I know you impulsive young fellows. You don't believe in polite preliminaries when you meet a girl who takes your fancy. You make a swan dive for her. You grab her. You start to kiss the stuffing out of her. And then what? She very properly scratches you to the bone, and serve you right. Let us hope that you will profit by this severe but very salutary lesson.'

'As a matter of fact, it was a ginger cat.'

'That's your story, is it? Thin, very thin. You'll have to do better than that, my lad.'

'It had got stuck up a tree –'

'Gadzooks!'

'– and a girl asked me to fetch it down.'

The austerity of Algy's demeanour had melted.

'Bill,' he said, 'I wronged you. I apologize unreservedly and withdraw my strictures. So you were the fathead who climbed that tree? My sister was telling me all about it.'

Bill started visibly.

'You don't mean that girl was your sister!'

'I believe she preens herself a good deal on the relationship. It gives her a *cachet* with her friends.'

'She doesn't look much like you.'

'No, poor soul, it's her secret sorrow. I wish I had a quid for every time she has gazed up at me with those blue eyes of hers and said "If only I could be big and strong and beautiful like you, Algy". Most unfortunate that she's such an undersized little microbe.'

Again Bill started noticeably. He spoke stiffly.

'She didn't strike me as an undersized little microbe.'

'Bit of a midget, surely? More like a half-sister than a sister. But a thoroughly nice girl, mind you. None better. Yes, Jane's all right.'

'Is that her name?'

'That's it.'

'Jane,' murmured Bill reverently, rolling the word round his tongue like vintage port. 'Is she often down this way?'

'Unlikely to come again. She's living in the country with my Uncle Henry, the original proprietor of that fiver.'

'Whereabouts in the country?'

'Ashby Hall, Ashby Paradene, Sussex.'

'Ashby Hall, Ashby Paradene, Sussex,' said Bill thoughtfully. He did not need to jot the address down in his notebook. He knew he would be able to remember it. It was printed on his mental eye in letters of flame.

For love had come to Bill Hardy this summer day. To keep

the record straight, it had come to him two or three times before in the course of his career, but those episodes, he could see now, had been mere boyish fancies.

This was the real thing.

Chapter Three

1

And now the minstrel, tuning his harp, prepares to sing of J. Wendell Stickney.

The only son of the late G. J. Stickney of Stickney's Dairy Products, he lived with his Aunt Kelly and his English valet Clarkson in an apartment at the upper end of Park Avenue, an address he was well able to afford, for his father had been just the sort of tycoon Jane had spoken of and had left him a fortune which would have satisfied even Algy at his most ambitious. And Henry had been right in supposing him to be the cultured dilettante type. Except for clipping coupons, he took no part in the world of finance. Commerce had no attraction for him.

At the moment when he enters this chronicle he was in his study digesting the excellent dinner provided by Heavenly Rest Johnson, his non-resident cook, and while waiting for Clarkson to bring coffee was reading a slim pamphlet entitled International Art Market, describing itself as a monthly report on current world prices of Art, antique furniture and *objets d'art*. The item in it that had arrested his attention was an announcement by the Messrs Sotheby of London that they were offering for sale a French eighteenth-century paperweight alluded to as follows:

109. CLICHY DOUBLE OVERLAY weight, turquoise, enclosing a well-formed mushroom, purple and white striped exterior, three concentric rows of pink, blue and green hollow canes, centred by a pink rose within a ring of white stardust canes, the sides cut with five circular windows and the top flattened by a large window, star-cut base.

To the normal man who reads mostly in order to find out

if it was the butler who did it, this little gem of English prose would have made small appeal. One pictures him yawning. But its effect on Mr Stickney was very different. It plainly spoke to his depths. His rather pale eyes glowed behind their tortoiseshell-rimmed spectacles, his breathing quickened and he registered a resolve to get in touch immediately with his agent in London.

For the conjectures of Henry and Jane as to the nature of his collection had been wide of the mark. Not old china, not first editions, not stamps or pictures or tropical fish. Wendell Stickney collected French eighteenth-century paperweights.

When a man spends a great deal of time and a great deal of money acquiring objects which most of his friends and acquaintances would not accept as a gift, it is always interesting to find out how he got that way, and one wishes one had more data relevant to Wendell Stickney's addiction to the habit of paying out large sums for the type of paperweight manufactured by the French in the eighteenth century. It is known that his earliest specimens were bequeathed to him by his godfather (who also collected gold and enamel Carl Fauberge parasol handles), and one assumes that he began adding to these from time to time in a desultory way, thinking, as so many collectors have thought, that just one more would not hurt him and that he could pull himself up whenever he pleased.

But it was the old, old story. A man tells himself that he can take French eighteenth-century paperweights or leave them alone, but comes a moment when he finds that he is hooked. Such a moment had long since come to Wendell. Nowadays he did not even try to resist the craving. French eighteenth-century paperweights were in his blood. He could not see one or even read about one without coveting it.

He was re-reading the Messrs Sotheby's remarks on mushrooms, circular windows and star-cut bases, lingering over each golden word, when his concentration was broken in upon by sounds of mirth from the passage outside his study door. He recognized the silvery notes of his Aunt Kelly and mingling with them the deeper guffaws of Mrs Heavenly Rest Johnson. Presently the front door slammed, indicating the departure of the latter for her native Harlem, and his aunt, relict of the late Theodore Stickney, came into the room.

In appearance Kelly was on the buxom side. In her middle forties she still retained much of the spectacular beauty of her youth, but a carelessness these last years in the matter of counting the calories had robbed her figure of its old streamlined look. Today she resembled a Ziegfeld Follies girl who had been left out in the rain and had swollen a little. She had very fine eyes, at the moment alight with amusement. Heavenly Rest, she said, had just told her the funniest story, and Mr Stickney quivered with austere disapproval. He had often had occasion to deplore in her this tendency to hobnob with the lower orders. He yielded to no one in his appreciation of Mrs Johnson's cooking, particularly her fried chicken Southern style, but he considered her an unsuitable intimate for one who, if only by marriage, was a Stickney. If she had funny stories to tell, he felt, let her tell them in the privacy of her own circle.

'It's about her brother-in-law Ephraim –'

'I don't want to hear it,' said Wendell.

It was a brusque remark and not unnaturally created a temporary silence, occupied by Mr Stickney in musing on this aunt of his and wishing that she conformed more closely to the code of a family which had always prided itself on its irreproachable correctness. That she was kind and jolly and good-hearted he conceded, but there was no denying that she lacked polish and had not even a rudimentary sense of her social position. He shared the opinion of his sister Mrs Loretta Stickney Pound, the well-known lecturer and publicist, that in marrying into the chorus his uncle Theodore had made the crowning mistake of a life which had always been open to criticism.

Furthermore, he had the uneasy feeling that one never knew when her impulsive nature might not lead her into some course of action which would make the fair name of Stickney a hissing and a byword. This fear also haunted his sister Loretta. Mark my words, Wendell, she had said not once but many times, one of these days that woman is going to get herself Into The Papers. And every time she said it Wendell had an unpleasant shuddery sensation in the pit of his stomach, as if some unfriendly hand had stirred up his vital organs with an egg whisk.

Kelly was much too genial a soul to be discouraged by a re-buff. Always interested in what other people were doing, she asked him what he was reading, and he said a catalogue.

'About paperweights?'

'About French eighteenth-century paperweights, yes.'

'Interesting?'

'Extremely.'

'Good. Will you be all right if I go out for a spell?'

'Perfectly, perfectly.'

'It's so darned hot I thought I'd take one of those hansom cabs outside the Plaza and drive around the Park for awhile.'

'An excellent idea,' said Mr Stickney. He could never help feeling a little nervous when she went out by herself, it being always possible that she would fraternize with someone quite undesirable, but she could hardly get into trouble alone in a hansom cab.

2

To his friends it was something of a mystery why a man like Wendell should share his home with an aunt by marriage like his Aunt Kelly, but the explanation was really very simple. She filled up the spare bedroom. If he had not acted promptly and installed her there, his sister Loretta would infallibly have moved in, and the mere thought of that chilled him to the marrow. She had been talking of doing so, reasoning that it was absurd to be paying the rent of two apartments when they could live so much more economically in one, and he had reached out for his aunt as a drowning swimmer reaches out for a life belt. Kelly might have her defects – he still frowned at the thought of her exchanging improper stories with Heavenly Rest Johnson – but she was not Mrs Loretta Stickney Pound.

Clarkson came in with the coffee, and a pleasant hour or more passed. Solitude always soothed Wendell. He read further in his *International Art Market*, decided to dispatch a cable to his London agent instructing him to bid for the paper-weight it had mentioned, and dozed off for perhaps twenty minutes. He woke to find that Clarkson had returned and was removing his coffee cup and at that moment the telephone rang. He jerked a thumb at it. He disliked talking on the telephone.

'If that's for me, say I'm out.'

Clarkson took up the receiver and cooed into it in his gentlemanly way.

'Mr Stickney's residence ... Oh, good evening, madam ... Indeed, madam? ... I see, madam ... How very disturbing, madam ... Yes, madam ... Quite, madam ... I will inform Mr Stickney immediately, madam ... That was madam, sir,' said Clarkson, removing the last trace of uncertainty his employer might have had. 'She would be glad if you would lend her ten dollars.'

'Ten dollars?'

'For bail, sir.'

'For bail?'

If it occurred to Clarkson that his overlord was modelling his conversational style a little too closely on that of an echo in the Swiss mountains, he did not say so. Well-trained valets learn to curb their tongues. He merely said 'Yes, sir', and there was a tense silence, broken by an animal cry from Mr Stickney as the purport of his words suddenly penetrated.

'Do you mean – ?'

'Yes, sir. Madam is in custody.'

Mr Stickney made a low gurgling sound as if choking for breath. He was telling himself that he had always expected that some tragedy of this sort would happen some day to this deplorable aunt of his. Bitterly he realized that he had underestimated the perils that lurk in hansom cabs. On the evidence submitted they would seem to be high up on the list of the city's danger spots.

In a hollow voice he said:

'Did she say – ?'

'Sir?'

'Did she say why – ?'

'No, sir. Merely that she was in the hands of the police and

39

would be glad of ten dollars for bail. Would you wish me to convey the money to madam?'

'Of course, of course.'

'Very good, sir.'

'Take a cab.'

'Yes, sir.'

'Did she say where – ?'

'I have the address, sir.'

'Then hurry.'

'Yes, sir.'

Clarkson melted away in the liquid fashion peculiar to English valets, and Wendell sank back into the chair from which he had sprung and gave himself up to sombre meditation. He was thinking of headlines in the tabloids, blazoning the family name in their largest type.

He was still shuddering as they rose before him, when the door flew open as if hit by one of those hurricanes which do so much to enliven the month of September for the population of the United States, and there entered the aunt on whom his thoughts were dwelling. Her face was red, her eyes flashed fire, and her general appearance was that of a woman who with some difficulty has managed to escape from a train wreck.

3

'All right, all right, all right!' she began immediately on her entry, her intention plainly to forestall hostile criticism. 'You're going to say you're shocked and surprised and horrified and you never heard of such a thing in your life, but let me tell you what happened and you'll agree that I was as innocent as a new-born babe. By the way, thanks for the ten.'

'Not at all,' said Wendell weakly. He was finding his relative by marriage a little overpowering. Normally she was the placid type, and he had never seen her in the grip of a powerful emotion.

'Yessir, innocent as a new-born babe.'

'You were about to tell me what happened.'

'Or a babe unborn, if you'd rather. There's not much in it.'

'Aunt Kelly!'

'Hello?'

'What *happened*?'

'You may well ask.'

Wendell reminded her that he had asked, and she seemed to see his point.

'Well,' she said, becoming calmer, 'it started with me not taking that hansom cab. I changed my mind. It was such a fine night that I thought I'd go to Coney Island.'

'Coney Island!' echoed Wendell, speaking in a low voice. He was aware that there were people who went there, but only, he had always understood, the proletariat. No Stickney had ever been guilty of such lower-class behaviour. Except possibly his Uncle Theodore in his hot youth. Uncle Theodore had done a number of things in the course of his career at which the family shook their heads. There was a story current that he liked to watch baseball from the bleachers and had more than once thrown a pop bottle at an umpire whose ruling had dissatisfied him.

'But I didn't get there. On account of what happened on the train.'

'Something happened on the train?'

'I'll say! And it wasn't my fault, either. Ask anybody who was there and they'll tell you that it wasn't me that started the fuss. There I was, minding my own business as innocent as a babe un –'

'Aunt Kelly!'

'Hello?'

'*What* happened on the train?'

'I'm telling you, if you'll only listen. Here's the set-up. Across the aisle from me there was a couple that seemed to be having some sort of husband and wife argument, but I wasn't paying much attention. He was shouting at her, and she was yelling at him, all perfectly normal. I scarcely gave them a glance. And then all of a sudden he slapped her.'

'Good gracious!' said Wendell, shivering. If a Stickney had

ever slapped anyone, the incident was certainly not recorded in the family archives.

'Well, then naturally I felt that it was time somebody did something about it. You can't have fellows slapping their wives even on a Coney Island train where a certain licence is always permitted. I stepped across and told the man he ought to be ashamed of himself, and he made a remark I hadn't heard since I was in the chorus.'

'Go on,' said Wendell faintly.

'So then I conked him with my bag, and let me tell you,' said Kelly, rightly interpreting her nephew's soft moan as a criticism of this policy, 'that if Queen Victoria had been there and had heard what this guy called me, she'd have done the same thing.'

Wendell's adam's apple moved convulsively.

'Go on,' he whispered.

'Well, what happened then you'll find it difficult to believe. Something suddenly hit me on the side of the head, and it was the woman's bag. Yessir, that's what it was, it was the bag of the identical broad I was battling on behalf of. Makes you feel there's no such thing as gratitude in the world.'

'And then?'

'Well, then the balloon went up. The next moment we were all conking each other, and bystanders took sides and joined in and the action became what you might call general. And most unfortunately there happened to be a couple of cops in the car where we were and they mixed in and scooped up as many of us as they could manage, and the next thing I knew I was in the pokey. I should mention that in the course of the proceedings my bag flew open and everything spilled out of it, which was why I had to come to you for that ten.'

For the first time since the narrative had begun Wendell brightened a little. It would be too much to say that even now he was tranquil, but he seemed to have detected something in the nature of a silver lining in the clouds.

'So they could not look in your bag and establish your identity?'

'No, everything was scattered all over the floor.'

'There were no letters addressed to you that they might have found?'

'I keep telling you that even if the cops had crawled around on all fours collecting the debris, they wouldn't have been able to sort out what belonged to who.'

'Ah!' said Wendell. It was a sigh of relief. In the final issue the luck of the Stickneys had held.

'Anyway, there weren't any letters in my bag, only a lipstick and a compact and a cigarette case and all like that. Say, talking of letters reminds me. One of yours got mixed up with mine this morning, and I forgot to give it to you. It's in my room. Who's Henry Paradene? Lives at a place called Ashby Hall in England.'

A reverent note came into Wendell's voice.

'Henry Paradene is the head of my family.'

'Then why isn't his name Stickney?'

'I belong to one of the collateral branches.'

'Whatever that means, if anything.'

'The Stickneys intermarried with the Paradenes in the early nineteenth century. But I can't explain now. What did he say?'

'He wants you to go over there and visit him.'

'How very gratifying!'

'Will you go?'

'Of course I shall go.'

'Then I'll come with you.'

'Impossible!'

'Why? If you were married, he'd expect you to take your wife along. Not being married, you bring your aunt. When do we start?'

For some moments Wendell sat plunged in thought. Distasteful as was the idea of introducing his Aunt Kelly into the refined surroundings of Ashby Hall, there was another more distasteful still. That was the idea of leaving her alone in New York with all the unexampled opportunities provided by that city for getting deposited in the pokey, this time with documents to identify her. Whatever excesses she might commit in England and however often the English police might take her into their custody, the Press of the island kingdom would surely not think her worth more than a brief paragraph at the bottom of one of the inside pages. He replied that it was his intention to start as soon as possible.

'You really want to come?'

'You couldn't stop me with an injunction.'

'Well, be careful.'

'How do you mean careful?'

'I was thinking of those stories of yours. Please, please do not tell stories like those when you are at Ashby Hall. These old English families are so particular.'

'Not even the one about Heavenly Rest's brother-in-law Ephraim? All right, just as you say. If that's how you want it. But they'll be missing some first class entertainment.'

Chapter Four

1

The clock over the Ashby Hall stables struck five, and almost simultaneously Jane, sitting in a deck chair on the lawn, saw the station taxi turn in at the great gates and come clattering up the drive with her Uncle Henry inside it. He had gone to London to lunch with Mr Stickney, who had suggested that it would be an excellent thing for them to get acquainted before he settled in.

As always when he had to dress up to go to London, Henry had been full of weak complainings and pleas that he be allowed to call the whole thing off, but Jane had been firm and he had departed, feeling, he said, as he had felt in the old days when sent for by a manager. Now, as he joined Jane on the lawn, he was his cheerful self again. He had, it appeared, enjoyed his lunch.

'A banquet,' he said. 'Stickney did us proud.'

'Us?' said Jane, surprised at his use of the royal or editorial pronoun.

'He's brought his aunt with him.'

'Oh, no!'

'Why the dismay?'

'It's a disaster. We aren't equipped to entertain rich American women. They expect something lavish.'

'Well, we've got a butler, a cook, a housemaid and a parlour-maid, and I doubt if they can beat that at Buckingham Palace. But I don't think she's rich. I put her down as a poor relation. And even if she's rolling in money she won't sneer at us. She's much too good a sort. Do you ever read Chaucer's Canterbury Tales?'

'Well, with one thing and another ... Why?'

'She reminds me of his Wife of Bath. Breezy and uninhibited. She used to be on the stage.'

'That sounds all right.'

'In the chorus. Most entertaining woman. She gave me the impression of knowing all the off-colour stories that ever went the rounds. There was one about her cook's brother-in-law Ephraim –'

He broke off. Inside the house the telephone was ringing. A few moments later Ferris, the butler, came out.

Ferris was large, ponderous and gloomy. He seemed always to be brooding on something, probably the cosmos, and not to be thinking very highly of it. As Henry had said more than once since his arrival, his spiritual home would have been some such establishment as Edgar Allen Poe's House of Usher, into which he would have fitted like the paper on the wall. It was in the sepulchral accents of a butler whom melancholy has long since marked for her own that he now spoke.

'A Mr Tarvin, miss, inquiring for you.'

'Tell him you couldn't find me.'

'Very good, miss,' said Ferris, and withdrew with clouded brow.

'Tarvin?' said Henry. 'Why does that name seem to ring a bell?'

'I was telling you about him. The man Lionel brought along to lunch.'

'Of course. Now I remember. Fellow with a beard.'

'That's right. Side-whiskers, too.'

'Why's he phoning you?'

'Ah, that we shall never know, unless he's left a message.'

Ferris reappeared, and Henry watched his approach with a critical eye.

'I've been wondering,' he said.

'Wondering what?'

'Why, when I sent you out hunting for butlers, you didn't pick one who occasionally looks on the bright side.'

'His dignity impressed me, and I thought it would impress Mr Stickney. Would you have preferred a gay, sprightly butler?'

'On the whole,' Henry admitted, 'no. I wouldn't want one who slid down the bannisters. Yes, Ferris?'

'Mr Tarvin expressed his regret, miss, that you were not available and desired me to tell you that he was sending you some good books.'

'Thank you, Ferris.'

'Thank you, miss,' said Ferris, and retired once more with the sombre step of one pacing behind the coffin of an old and valued friend.

'What's Tarvin sending you good books for?' asked Henry, and Jane laughed.

'To improve my mind. I thought something like this might happen. We got on to the subject of books at lunch, and he wanted to know what my favourite reading was. I told him novels of suspense. Do you remember one I gave you the other day called *Deadly Ernest*? By some woman, I forget her name. It had me spellbound.'

'Me, too. I couldn't put it down. Which reminds me. I promised to lend it to the vicar.'

'Does he read novels of suspense?'

'He loves them.'

'And he's a ripe scholar who writes solid stuff about the early Church Fathers. I wish I'd known that when I was talking to Tarvin. You see, when I recommended *Deadly Ernest* to him as required reading, he snubbed me in no uncertain manner.'

'What's he like when snubbing?'

'Pretty formidable. The beard helps a lot, of course. He waggled it at me and said "Dear lady, does one read books called *Deadly Ernest*?" And when I said Yes, one did, mentioning myself as a case in point, he sighed like a patronizing escape of steam and said he was afraid my taste was very crude. What a pity I couldn't hurl the vicar in his teeth. I wonder what he's sending: Probably something educational. Do you know what, Henry? I've suddenly got on to it. He's moulding me.'

'Absurd. You're perfect as you are.'

'That's what I think, too. But he's moulding me all right. The signs are all there.'

'It's always a mistake to mould people. It only gets their backs up. They did it to me at school and after that at Cambridge. And when I came down from Cambridge and went on the stage, blowed if it didn't start all over again with directors and choreographers. Do you think Stickney will try to mould me?'

'I wouldn't be surprised. What's he like?'

'Quite a good chap, I thought. A bit on the prim side. I have an idea he didn't altogether approve of his aunt as a raconteuse. I saw him looking rather bleak as she told her tales. With great tact I eased the situation by saying I had heard he was a collector. He never stopped talking after that. And we were wrong about his collecting, Jane. You won't believe me, but what he likes are paperweights. French eighteenth-century paperweights, to be exact.'

'Oh, those?'

'You speak as if they were familiar to you.'

'Of course they are. You've got one.'

'I have?'

'Certainly. The Beau brought it back from the grand tour in eighteen hundred and something. I'm one of its warmest admirers. It's up in the picture gallery with the other heirlooms.'

Henry winced. She had touched an exposed nerve.

'Don't talk to me about those heirlooms. I hate them. When I reflect how much they're worth and remember that the law won't let me sell them, the iron enters into my soul. What would a French eighteenth-century paperweight fetch, do you think? Don't bother to answer, for of course you haven't a notion.'

'As it happens, I have. I was reading about it in the paper. One was sold at Christie's the other day for a thousand pounds.'

Henry uttered a stricken cry.

'A thousand? Good God! Now you really have spoiled my day. There's that one of mine sitting on its fanny up in the picture gallery, worth all that money, and no hope of cashing in on it. Just because some ass made this law barring the sale of heirlooms. It's maddening. If only I had a thousand pounds –'

'You're just like Algy.'

'When you say that, smile. And please don't talk of Algy. It does something to my blood pressure.'

'No, tell me about Mr Stickney.'

'There isn't much to tell. He's trying to knock off smoking, and he's fond of good wine, of which, thank goodness, I have plenty, thanks to the liberality of the Messrs Duff and Trotter. So ... What's the matter?'

Jane had uttered a sharp cry.

'Oh, Henry, I clean forgot.'

'Forgot what?'

'About Algy and the broker's man.'

'Good Lord! Don't tell me Algy's had the brokers in?'

'Yes, and do you know where this one came from? Duff and Trotter, the people you owe all that money to. You don't think they'll send one here? It would be too awful if a mob of brokers' men came charging in just when you were on the point of selling the house to Mr Stickney. It would put him right off.'

Henry with his customary airiness refused to allow any such possibility to disturb him. It was never easy to make him take the gloomy view. His attitude towards the future was always the old theatrical one that it would be all right on the night.

'Don't let the thought worry you for a moment, my dear girl. You can't go by what happens to Algy. A respectable firm like Duff and Trotter doesn't play that sort of trick on people like me. I'm a hell of a fellow with a quarter of a page in *Burke's Landed Gentry*. They'd be scared that I'd raise my eyebrows at them. There's that telephone.'

Jane rose.

'Probably Tarvin again.'

She was gone for quite some little time. On her face, when she returned, there was a happy smile.

'Guess what,' she said.

'Was it Tarvin?'

'Not this time. Algy.'

'What did he want?'

'He asked me if I knew anyone who would lend him five hundred pounds. He's got one of his big schemes on, and needs capital.'

'Bless his heart. He didn't suggest me?'

'No, even Algy isn't so optimistic as that,' said Jane.

2

His brow knit in a frown, Wendell Stickney sat on the low wall of the terrace outside the front door of Ashby Hall, but he was not frowning because that peculiar relic of the Regency days offended his aesthetic sense. His thoughts were elsewhere. He was musing on French eighteenth-century paperweights and in particular on the one his host's niece had shown him when taking him for a tour of the house after dinner last night.

He wanted that paperweight. He yearned for it and was quite willing to pay a high price if its owner could be induced to part with it.

But could he? That was the question which he was asking himself as he sat on the terrace wall. These English aristocrats, he knew, were apt to be touchy and to take offence if you brought business into the conversation. Make a wrong move, and you were lucky if you did not get the cold 'Well, really!' or the even colder 'Most extraordinary', coupled with the glacial British stare and the raised British eyebrow.

He would probably have continued to muse in this strain indefinitely, but at this moment a hearty voice hailed him and he turned to see his Aunt Kelly.

'Hi, Wendell,' she said. 'What are you doing, perched there like a buzzard on a rock?'

The imagery did not please Wendell greatly, but he replied in a reasonably courteous voice that he had been thinking and asked how she had been occupying herself.

'Hank's been showing me around the grounds. You ought to go take a look at them. There's a lake through those trees about as big as the one in Central Park. One of his ancestors had it put in. Must have cost a fortune.'

'That would no doubt have been the notorious Beau Paradene,' said the well-informed Wendell. 'He was noted for his extravagances.'

'So Hank was telling me.'

At the repetition of the name Wendell gave a little start.

'You are speaking of Mr Paradene?'

'Who else?'

'You don't *call* him Hank?'

'Sure. I asked him if I could. We both agreed that it was snappier than Henry.'

'You mean that you are on those intimate terms already?'

'We're like ham and eggs.'

'Then,' said Wendell, 'there is something you can do for me. When Miss Martyn was showing me the house last night –'

He left the sentence incompleted. Jane had come out on to the terrace.

3

Jane was in cheerful mood. Her apprehensions concerning visiting American women had been dissipated within five minutes of Kelly's arrival. The relict of the late Theodore Stickney made friends easily.

'Hullo there,' she said. 'I'm off to the village to get tobacco for Henry. Do you need any, Mr Stickney?'

'Thank you, I do not smoke. I used to, but I have given it up.'

'He eats candy,' said Kelly. 'He likes those squashy chocolate bars.'

'I'll get some. Would you care to come to the village, Mrs Stickney?'

'Call me Kelly.'

'May I?'

'I'll be wounded if you don't. How far is it?'

'About a mile.'

'And a mile back. I can see myself. I'll walk down the drive with you. Tell me,' said Kelly, as they moved off, 'do you like living all the time in the country? Not that I'm knocking it. I think it's swell. But I'd have thought you'd feel kind of buried.'

'Oh, I'm only spending my holiday here. I work in London. I'm a secretary.'

'Well, what do you know about that! I was one myself before I went into the chorus. Afterwards, too, when I got too heavy for the dance routines and the managers didn't seem to want me. That was how I met Theodore.'

'Theodore?'

'My late husband. The concern I worked for sent me to him to take dictation. He'd been quite a lad about town in his day and he was writing his reminiscences. And there was a lot of the old pep in him still. Do you know those Peter Arno drawings in the *New Yorker*?'

'Of course.'

'He was like one of those. Grey moustache and all that, and plenty of get-up. I went to his apartment and we got on fine. In fact, it was only about a week before he was asking me to marry him. How well I remember that day. He was having one of his spells of indigestion. He got them quite a good deal, poor lamb, and used to take brandy for them. Said he'd been advised to by a friend of his who claimed it was the only thing to do. He's dead now. The friend, I mean. Cirrhosis of the liver. Ah well, all flesh is grass, as the fellow said. And that afternoon he may well have taken just that one snifter too many which makes all the difference, because right in the middle of a reminiscence about the old Haymarket he suddenly started chasing me around the table. And to cut a long story short, the next thing I knew he'd got a half-Nelson on me and was kissing me like a ton of bricks.'

She paused, her mind back in the golden past.

'Tell me more,' said Jane.

'Well, of course I conked him.'

'Of course.'

'With a paperweight, which was an odd coincidence when you come to think of it because those are what Wendell collects. Daffy it's always seemed to me, though I once knew a guy who collected match boxes. Hundreds of them he'd got, all different. Well, when I say match boxes, I mean those paper ones. He used to wander around town trying to find some beanery where they'd have their own specials. I often say it takes all sorts to make a world. Where was I?'

'Conking Mr Theodore Stickney with a paperweight.'

'Oh, yes. Well, they say Heaven protects the working girl, and maybe they're right, but it doesn't do any harm if she lends a hand herself. Can't leave everything to the men up top. I let him have it with plenty of follow-through, and while he was rubbing his head he explained that I had got him all wrong. He hadn't meant it that way, he said, he wanted me to be his wife, to look after him in his declining years. He said he had had me taped from the first as a girl with a gentle, womanly heart. You see, in between taking dictation about the old days in New York I used to rub his tummy when his indigestion acted up, and that kind of impressed him, if you know what I mean.'

'I can see how it would have.'

'So we got engaged. The family put up a considerable beef when it was announced, of course, and I don't blame them, because I wasn't everybody's dream girl and they thought Theodore was blotting the what's that thing you blot?'

'The escutcheon?'

'Is that it? Escutcheon sounds to me like some kind of fish. Well, whatever it's called, they said he was blotting it the worst way. But it didn't get them anywheres. We were married a week later at the Little Church Around The Corner, and very happy we were, too, till he got that apoplectic stroke and passed on. You couldn't keep the poor angel off the lobster Newburg and caviare, and of course the brandy helped quite a good deal. But, as I say, everything was fine while he lasted. You hear people knocking married life, but it suited me. Are you planning to get married?'

'I'm engaged.'

'Boy next door?'

'No, a man in London.'

'What's his line?'

'He's an interior decorator.'

'You're kidding.'

'No, that's what he is.'

'Then ditch him.'

'What!'

'Ditch him,' said Kelly firmly. 'I was once engaged to an interior decorator, so I speak as one who knows. They're the scum of the earth.'

Jane laughed.

'That's what my brother says. I think Henry feels that way, too, only he's too polite to say so.'

At the mention of Henry a thoughtful look had come into Kelly's face.

'This Hank routine,' she said, 'I don't get it.'

'What's puzzling you?'

'The whole set-up. He told me he used to be on the stage. How did he suddenly change from a ham into a lord of the manor, if that's what you call it?'

'Oh, that? Very simple. One or two relations ahead of him on the list died, and he was the next in line. He just inherited.'

'Like princes do when kings hand in their dinner pails?'

'Exactly.'

Kelly pondered over this for a moment or two.

'Well, I guess it's all right if he likes it,' she said at length, 'but he must get pretty lonesome living by himself out here in the styx all the year around.'

Jane relieved her mind.

'It's not so bad as all that. He has plenty of friends here. He's very popular.'

'I'm not surprised,' said Kelly with warmth. 'Hank's a swell guy. They don't come any better.'

'He's dining somewhere tonight, as a matter of fact. He asked me to tell you and make his apologies for leaving you. He said he couldn't get out of it.'

'All right by me.'

'It's at Mr Wade-Pigott's, that big house across the valley. He's on the Stock Exchange. I think it's his birthday or something.'

'You going too?'

'Good heavens, no, they don't want me. It's an all-men affair. They sit and yarn and tell each other Stock Exchange stories.'

'They ought to let me join the gang one of these nights. I know more stories than you could shake a stick at. Well, here's where I leave you,' said Kelly as they reached the great iron gates and the cottage which had been the lodge keeper's in the days when Ashby Hall had been able to afford a lodge keeper. 'Don't forget Wendell's chocolate bars.'

She made her way to the terrace. Wendell was still sitting there, and seemed in peevish mood.

'I wish you would not go off like that when I wanted to talk to you,' he complained.

'What's on your mind?'

'I was starting to say that there was something I wish you would do for me. When Miss Martyn was taking me round the house, she showed me the most perfect French eighteenth-century paperweight I have ever seen. I must have it. I'll pay whatever Paradene wants for it.'

'We'll make him an offer.'

'I don't like to. He might take offence and snub me.'

'Not a regular fellow like Hank.'

'Possibly not. But I do not care to risk it. But as you and he have become on such friendly terms –'

'I get the message. You want me to act as your agent?'

'Precisely.'

'Consider it done,' said Kelly. The Stickney family might regard her as one who caused escutcheons to become blotted, but nobody had ever called her disobliging.

Chapter Five

1

When a young man with the right stuff in him learns that the girl with whom he has fallen in love at first sight is residing at Ashby Hall, Ashby Paradene, Sussex, he does not remain tamely in Burberry Road, Valley Fields, London S.E. 23, thinking of her from afar. As soon as possible he gets as near Ashby Hall as he can manage, in the hope of seeing something of her. Bill had done this, establishing himself at the Beetle and Wedge inn half-way along Ashby Paradene's High Street.

The passage of the days since their meeting in Burberry Road had done nothing to diminish Bill's conviction that in Algy's sister Jane he had found the girl he had been looking for all his life. It had, indeed, deepened it.

There are those who maintain that love should be a reasoned emotion. When a young man marries, they hold, it should be as the result of a carefully calculated process of thought. He should first decide after cool reflection that he had reached the age at which it is best for him to marry. He should then run over the list of his female friends till he has selected one whose mind and tastes are in harmony with his. Let him then watch her carefully for a considerable length of time in order to assure himself that he has not allowed passion to blind him to any faults in her disposition. After that, provided in the interval he has not found any more suitable candidate for his affections, he may go to her and in a few simple words ask her to be his wife. He will point out that his income is sufficient for two, that his morals are above reproach, that his disposition is amiable and his habits regular. They will then settle down to the Marriage Sane.

Admirable advice, of course, but if some well-meaning friend had tried it out on Bill, he would have had little hope of making a convert of him. What Bill wanted was rapid action. Theirs in Burberry Road had not been an extended encounter, but it had been long enough to enable him to gather that in addition to looking like a Tanagra statuette, Jane Martyn possessed all the qualities he most admired in woman. She could not have been constructed more in accordance with his specifications. And when he recalled that Algy had alluded to her as an undersized little microbe, his blood boiled briskly and his affection for his old friend suffered a temporary eclipse. One had, he told himself, always to make allowances for brothers where their sisters were concerned, but even so there were surely limits to the amount of drivel a brother was entitled to talk.

At this point in his meditations a thought not connected with Jane forced itself on his attention. Although under the influence of his great passion he had become practically pure spirit, there were moments when mundane matters intruded themselves, and one of these occurred as he sat smoking in the lounge of the Beetle and Wedge. He suddenly realized that if he did not soon replenish his stock, he would be running short of tobacco. He made this discovery some twenty minutes after Jane had parted from Kelly at the gates of Ashby Hall.

There was only one tobacconist in Ashby Paradene, and so it came about that just as he had put in his bid for half a pound of Brigg's Honeydew, Jane entered the shop with the object of buying a similar amount of Watson's Navy Cut for her Uncle Henry. They met at the counter.

Both expressed astonishment, though only Jane felt it. Optimistic by nature, Bill had been sure that Providence would arrange a meeting sooner or later. His sole criticism of Providence's handling of the matter was that he would have preferred it if that meeting could have taken place in some sylvan glade and not in a rather smelly tobacconist's emporium. Ashby Paradene did not believe in opening windows.

'Why, hullo!' said Jane, surprised.

'Good heavens!' said Bill, astounded.

'How very unexpected,' said Jane.

'Yes,' said Bill.

'So odd meeting you again like this.'

'Yes.'

'What brings you here?'

'I'm taking a country holiday.'

'Me, too. I'm staying with an uncle of mine at a place called Ashby Hall.'

'Oh, really?'

'I came to buy tobacco for him. Half a pound of Watson's Navy Cut, please, Mr Jellicoe. Are you staying long?'

'I'm not quite sure.'

'It's a pretty village.'

'Yes.'

'Are you at the Beetle and Wedge?'

'Yes.'

'Everybody says it's very comfortable.'

'Oh, it is.'

There was a pause. The conversation, to Bill's concern showed signs of flagging. He saw that he must make an effort to brighten it, or it would expire in its tracks.

'Have you met any interesting cats lately?' he asked.

He smiled as he spoke, and Jane, who had been thinking as she had thought at their former encounter, how closely he resembled something out of a gangster film, suddenly saw him as he was, a kindly and attractive young man obviously full of good will to one and all.

'Not up trees,' she said. 'Just to nod to when we meet in the house. There are three of them at my uncle's place. Two and a half, rather, because one of them is a kitten. How are your scratches getting on? Healing, I hope?'

'Oh, yes, thanks.'

'No lockjaw?'

'Not so far. It was rather funny. When Algy saw them –'

'Algy?'

'Your brother.'

Jane gave a surprised squeak. Very musical, Bill thought it. She stared incredulously.

'You know Algy?'

'We were at school together. He's living with me.'

'Good heavens! You aren't the Bill he talks about?'

'Yes.'

'Well, well! That legendary figure! Do you mind if I call you Bill?'

'I wish you would. Er – may I call you Jane?'

'I shall be wounded if you don't, as Kelly would say.'

'Kelly?'

'A guest at the Hall. American. Very good sort. By the way, did Algy give you that fiver?'

'Yes. I didn't want to take it, but he insisted.'

'Is he with you?'

'No, I left him at home. Extraordinary that you should turn out to be his sister.'

'Extraordinary that you should turn out to be his best friend and severest critic.'

'Yes, most extraordinary, the whole thing.'

There was a silence as they pondered on how extraordinary it all was. Jane was the first to break it.

'Has he shaved yet? He spoke of growing a beard.'

'Surely not even Algy – ?'

'I don't know so much. He might. Thank you,' said Jane, taking the half pound of Navy Cut which Mr Jellicoe, whom she greatly impressed, had been wrapping reverently in a parcel. 'And now for Mr Stickney's chocolate bars. He's an American millionaire who's staying at the Hall. Kelly's nephew. He munches them instead of smoking.'

The purchase of the chocolate bars completed, they came out into the street.

'Well,' said Jane, and she was so plainly about to add the word 'Goodbye' that Bill hastened to interrupt her. This conversation had confirmed him in the opinion that a single moment spent without her at his side would be a moment wasted.

'You're headed for home?' he said.

'I ought to be getting back. Mr Stickney is probably counting the minutes. You know what these chocolate bar addicts are like.'

'I'll walk with you, may I?'

'Haven't you a hundred important engagements?'

'In Ashby Paradene?'

'I see what you mean. Yes, do come. As a matter of fact, I want to have a serious talk with you. About Algy. He told me you had come into money. Correct?'

'Quite correct.'

'Then for heaven's sake don't let him borrow it for one of his schemes. Has he tried?'

'He did mention something about starting an Advice To the Lovelorn bureau.'

'I hope you were firm.'

'Oh, very.'

'He's always so frightfully plausible. He once talked my uncle into putting money into a play he'd written.'

'I didn't know Algy had written a play.'

'It never came to London. Died in Southsea or somewhere, and Uncle Henry several hundred pounds in the red. He shudders at the mention of Algy's name now and won't have him in the house.'

'Algy didn't tell me that.'

'Well, would he if he's hoping to get a subsidy from you? I love him like a brother, which he is of course, but –'

'I know what you mean by "but".'

'If he wants to dip into your millions, don't let him, no matter how good he makes it sound. Be adamant.'

'I will.'

'What do you plan to do with your wealth?'

'I was telling Algy. I'm going to settle down in the country somewhere.'

'What will you do there? Raise chickens?'

'Write.'

'Oh? Well, I suppose you know your own business best,' said Jane dubiously. 'I don't think I'd like to run a poultry farm myself.'

Bill saw that the intricacies of the English language had misled her.

'When I said write, I didn't mean right, I meant write,' he said helpfully.

'Oh, write?'

'Right.'

'I'm glad we've got that straight. It was worrying me. What are you going to write?'

'Anything that comes into my head. I'm not fussy.'

'Have you written much yet?'

'A few articles and a book.'

'A novel?'

'A thriller.'

'That's the spirit. I love thrillers. I read all I can get. What was it called?'

'*Deadly Ernest.*'

'What!'

'Ernest without an a,' said Bill, wondering, as so many authors have done, why the title of a book, spoken aloud, should always sound so fatuous and wrong. 'Ernest was the villain.'

'You don't have to tell me. He froze every red corpuscle in my body.'

Bill was amazed.

'You don't mean you read it!'

'At a sitting. I didn't buy it, I'm afraid. I work on a weekly paper, and the book critic gave me the review copy. I thought it was terrific. So did my uncle. We particularly liked its austerity.'

Bill blinked.

'It's what?'

'Or restraint, if you prefer it. No second corpse.'

'I thought of putting in a second corpse, and then I thought I'd fool my public by not having one.'

'You were quite right. I'm sick of second corpses. Are you going to write another?'

'Dozens, now that my time is my own.'

'Wasn't it always?'

'No, I had a job in the City and could only write at night. Writing at night after a hard day at the office is difficult.'

'I can imagine.'

They walked on in silence for awhile – a restful, comradely

silence. It seemed incredible to Bill that he should have found probably the only girl in the world who looked like an angel in human form and in addition was easy to talk to. Hitherto it had always seemed to him to be Nature's law that the photogenic of the other sex had nothing to say for themselves, while those with whom it was possible to exchange ideas were dumpy and wore spectacles.

'That book of yours,' said Jane. She appeared to have been thinking. 'If I remember, it had a female name attached to it. Angela something.'

'Adela Bristow.'

'Why?'

'Well, I couldn't very well use my own name.'

'Why not? What is your name?'

'Thomas Hardy.'

'Oh?'

'It might have caused confusion.'

'Yes, I see your difficulty. But why did Algy call you Bill?'

'Everybody always has, I don't know why. It started at school.'

'I still don't get the Adela Bristow. If Thomas Hardy had been used by someone else, why not George Hardy or Herbert Hardy or Algernon Hardy?'

'Oh, that was subtle strategy. I pictured a customer with a slight impediment in his speech going to a book shop and saying to the clerk "Gimme an Agatha Christie". Whereupon the clerk, who happens to be a little hard of hearing, slips him an Adela Bristow and it's wrapped up and the fellow has paid for it and taken it away and he doesn't spot the error till he has got home and it's too late. That sort of thing happening often enough could bump up the royalties quite a good deal. But mine remained small, and I think I know the reason why. What's wrong with the England of today is that there are too few deaf book shop clerks and not enough booklovers who speak indistinctly. I'm hoping conditions are better in America.'

'Have you sold it in America?'

'Not yet. But an agent there wrote to me saying he had read it and thought he could place it, so I'm keeping my fingers crossed. He's had it two or three weeks now, and I ought to be hearing from him soon.'

'Why, that's wonderful.'

'Promising, anyway. Good Lord,' said Bill, sighting the iron gates. 'Don't tell me we're there already. I thought we'd only just started.'

Jane, too, had found the time pass with a pleasant swiftness. There was a touch of regret as she spoke.

'Yes, this is the end of the line. Stop right here, or you'll see the house.'

'And you don't advise that?'

'It's not a thing you want to come on suddenly,' said Jane. 'Particularly to be avoided by nervous people and invalids.'

As she walked up the drive, she was asking herself if she ought not to have invited this excellent young man to come up to the Hall one of these afternoons and join the inmates at lunch. She decided that it would be better to consult Henry first. She found him sunning himself on the terrace and put this social problem to him.

'Here's your tobacco, Henry,' she said. 'And who do you think I met at the shop? The man I was telling you about who climbed the tree to get the cat. He also wrote that *Deadly Ernest* book you liked so much, and he's a friend of Algy's. Don't you think we ought to ask him to lunch? It's an impressive list of qualifications.'

Henry shook his head. He had his fixed rules and abided by them.

'Not a friend of Algy's,' he said firmly.

'But this one's respectable.'

'Outwardly, perhaps, but I can't take chances. Let a friend of his into the house and the next thing you know Algy would be popping in to see how he was getting on and trying to touch Stickney for money to put into his next play.'

'He may not write another play.'

'We can't fool ourselves with wishful thinking like that. And if it wasn't a play, it would be some scheme for getting gold out of sea water. No, if this man of yours wants lunch, let him buy his own.'

'Oh, all right. It was only a suggestion,' said Jane, and as she spoke Kelly came on to the terrace.

'Hank,' she said. 'Can I have a word with you?'

'I should enjoy it.'

'In private. Get lost, young Jane,' said Kelly, and Jane took the hint, mystified as to what all the secrecy was about.

2

In the Servants Hall at this moment Mr Stickney's valet Clarkson was in conversation over a glass of Duff and Trotter's port with Ferris, the butler. They had made the interesting discovery that they had been in service simultaneously in New York only half a dozen blocks from one another, and this had formed a bond which the port was rapidly cementing.

But if spiritually they were akin, physically there was a great difference between them. Ferris, if he had ever managed to get a mention in *Time*, would have been described as stout, rubicund, balding Andrew Ferris (54). Clarkson in sharp contradistinction was small, pale, skinny (36), and he had a head of lemon-coloured hair of which he was justly proud.

Silence had fallen as they sipped. Ferris had been musing, as was his habit when in thought, on Brangmarley Manor, Little-Seeping-In-The-Wold, Shropshire, where he had spent the early happy days of his butlerhood. It was Clarkson who was the first to resume the exchanges.

'How did you like it in America, Mr Ferris?'

'I disapproved of America.'

'Too much rush and bustle?'

'Precisely. I was in the employment of a Mr Waddington, and you would scarcely believe the goings-on there. Jewel robberies, girls bursting in at wedding ceremonies and accusing the bridegroom of having betrayed them, policemen in every nook and cranny. Matters reached such a pass that I was actually enrolled as a sheriff's deputy.'

'How was that?'

'It is a long story.'

'You must tell it to me some time.'

'Now, if you wish.'

'Not now, if it's long. I must be leaving you very shortly to go to the village and send a telegram. Did all this happen in New York?'

'No, at our country residence at Old Westbury. It upset me considerably, and I gave my notice. I was not sorry to do so, for I had found my colleagues at the Waterbury home most uncongenial.'

'What was wrong with them?'

'Several of them were Swedes, and the rest Irish.'

'You don't like Swedes?'

'I disapprove of them.'

'Why?'

'Their heads are too square.'

'And you disapprove of the Irish?'

'Precisely.'

'Why?'

'Because they are Irish.'

To Clarkson, some of whose best friends were Swedish and Irish, it occurred as a passing thought that his companion, however gifted at buttling, must have been a difficult man to fit in socially.

'They can't help being Irish,' he argued.

Ferris pursed his lips, as though affronted by this specious reasoning. He seemed to be thinking that they could if they tried. It only needed, his silence suggested, an effort. Clarkson tactfully changed the controversial subject.

'You are an observant man, Mr Ferris?'

'Why do you ask?'

'I was wondering if you'd noticed something rather interesting going on here.'

'I do not understand you.'

'Paradene and our Kelly.'

'I still fail to follow you.'

'I believe there's a romance starting there.'

'Indeed? What makes you think that?'

'The way they look at each other. I thought you'd have been bound to spot it. Give them a glance next time you bring in the drinks.'

'I very seldom give my employers a glance.'

'Well, you can take my word for it. I'm never mistaken about that sort of thing. And good luck to them, I say. He seems a good sort and she's one of the best, and I'd like to see her happily married.'

'If such a thing is possible, Mr Clarkson.'

His words jarred unpleasantly on Clarkson, who was a romantic. He was beginning to think that even Duff and Trotter's port could hardly compensate for having to listen to a man who held such subversive views.

'I hope you don't disapprove of marriage, Mr Ferris.'

'I do.'

'Are you married?'

'A widower.'

'Well, weren't you happy when you got married?'

'I was not.'

'Was Mrs Ferris?'

'She appeared to take a certain girlish pleasure in the ceremony, but it soon blew over.'

'How do you account for that?'

'I could not say, Mr Clarkson.'

'I should have thought when two people love each other and want to get married –'

'Marriage is not a process for prolonging the life of love. It merely mummifies the corpse.'

'But, Mr Ferris, if there were no marriages, what would become of posterity?'

'I see no necessity for posterity, Mr Clarkson.'

'You disapprove of it?'

'I do.'

Clarkson rose in a rather marked manner, as any man of sentiment would have done in his place. This butler's views on love, a subject to which he had given much thought from his earliest years, revolted him. If it was wrong of him to label Ferris in his mind as a potbellied old codfish who talked through the back of his neck, he must be forgiven, for he was much moved.

'Well, I must be off to the village,' he said, 'and I suppose I'd better go and get permission. It isn't strictly necessary, but one likes to do the civil thing.'

3

When Jane had left them, Kelly wasted no time in coming to the point. She did not believe in beating about bushes. With no preliminary preamble she said:

'How are you fixed for lettuce, Hank?'

'You want to make a salad?'

Kelly clicked her tongue impatiently. As Clarkson had observed, she was beginning to entertain for Henry what are called feelings deeper and warmer than those of ordinary friendship, but she found him slow at times.

'Dough. Cash. Glue. Coin of the realm. Money.'

'Oh, money? I couldn't think what you meant. How much do you want?'

'I don't want any. This isn't a touch.'

'That's a relief, because I'm rather short at the moment.'

'Exactly what I was trying to find out. Now we can go ahead. Suppose someone were to offer you a thousand pounds, whatever that is in dollars, how would you react?'

Henry had no difficulty in answering this.

'I'd faint. And when I came to, I should probably kiss him. Wouldn't it be wonderful if there were lunatics like that around.'

'There are. Wendell for one.'

'He doesn't strike me as unbalanced.'

'On his special subject he's as nutty as a fruit cake. Throw your mind back to that lunch where I first met you. Remember how after contributing practically nil to the conversation he suddenly opened up and started spouting like the Old Faithful geyser when you asked him what he collected?'

'Yes, I remember that.'

'He's always that way when he gets talking about paperweights. If they're French eighteenth-century, I mean. What he sees in the darned things beats me, but there it is. He particularly admires that one of yours.'

'Mine? Which one of mine? I haven't got a French eighteenth-century paperweight. I'm proud to say.'

'You do, too, have one. Young Jane showed it to Wendell.'

'By Jove, yes, you're perfectly right. I'd forgotten.'

'And Wendell was raving to me just now about it being the most perfect specimen he had ever seen. What makes one lousy paperweight better than another lousy paperweight I couldn't tell you, but that's what he said, and he asked me to sound you about selling it to him. He'll probably go as high as a thousand pounds for it. Is it a deal? Think on your feet.'

If Henry was doing this, it was plain from the look of anguish which contorted his face that the thoughts he was thinking were not agreeable ones. His jaw had fallen, and there had come into his eyes the sadness one sees in those of a bear in a Zoo when the child who is extending a bun in its direction has second thoughts and withdraws it.

'Blast!' he said, finding speech. 'Damn!' he added. 'Oh, hell!' he concluded, and Kelly eyed him inquiringly.

'What's all that about?' she asked in some bewilderment. It had not been the reaction she had expected.

At this moment Wendell joined them. He had been lurking in the house, trying to wait in patience for the outcome of his agent's negotiations, and now he felt that he had given her all the time she could reasonably require.

'Oh, Aunt Kelly,' he said. 'Have you spoken to Paradene about – er – that?'

To the lay mind the question might have seemed obscure, but Kelly had no difficulty in interpreting his meaning. She replied that that was precisely what she had been doing.

'I put it up to him a minute ago, and he's only just stopped swearing.'

For the first time Wendell observed Henry's agitation, and he sighed despondently. It was, he was telling himself, just as he had feared. The sordid note of commerce having been struck, the haughty English aristocrat had taken umbrage. He was about to frame an apology, coupled with a promise that nothing of this description would ever happen again, when Henry became coherent.

'I'm sorry,' he said. 'I'm terribly sorry. The reason I cursed a trifle was that there's nothing I'd like better than to sell the thing, but I can't.'

'You can't?' said Kelly, bewildered.

'No.'

'How come? It's yours, isn't it?'

'No.'

'*Not* yours?' Kelly seemed shocked. 'Are you telling me that you've got your hooks on a hot paperweight?'

'It's an heirloom.'

'What's an heirloom?'

'Haven't you ever heard of heirlooms?'

'Never.'

'Or entails?'

'Nor those. Nobody tells me anything.'

Wendell with his wider knowledge took it upon himself to explain. He did it in a voice which disappointment rendered hollow. Henry's words had blotted the sunshine from his life. He had set his heart on the Beau's paperweight.

'I am afraid I know what Paradene means,' he said. 'In old English families certain objects of value pass from the ownership of the head of the family to his heir and from the heir to *his* heir and so on. And unless the entail is broken no temporary owner can dispose of them. These are called heirlooms. Do I make myself clear?'

'No,' said Kelly.

Henry came to Wendell's assistance.

'It's perfectly simple, really. If there's an entail, the damn things have to stay put. Do *I* make myself clear?'

'Not so you would notice it,' said Kelly. 'It all sounds looney to me.'

Henry continued patient, like a kindly tutor elucidating some difficult point to a dull pupil.

'Well, take me, for instance. When I inherited this house, the paperweight went with it. The bloke who had it before me wasn't allowed to sell it. I'm not allowed to sell it. Whoever comes after me won't be allowed to sell it. Ashby Hall is stuck with it as long as there's a Paradene family. We may all go broke, our children may cry for bread and starve to death, but we can't raise money on the paperweight. Now do you see?'

Kelly was beginning to, if only dimly. The whole set-up appeared to her about as cockeyed as a set-up could be, but she was able to recognize that it existed. It was, she felt resignedly, the sort of thing one had to expect in England, like driving on the left and calling Cholmondeley Marchbanks.

'What would happen if you did sell it?'

'I'd get jugged. It's against the law to sell an heirloom.'

'Suppose someone pinched it?'

'That would be different.'

'You wouldn't go up the river then?'

'Of course not.'

'Then why not have Wendell pinch it?' said Kelly. 'Then he would have his little old paperweight and you would have your thousand smackers and everybody would be happy.'

Silence followed the simultaneous gasps which this simple outline of strategy had caused to proceed from the lips of her audience. Wendell's emotion was caused by the thought, which he had had several times since his arrival at Ashby Hall, that it had been a grave mistake to introduce so deplorable an aunt into these refined surroundings. Henry, on the other hand, had gasped with admiration of this woman's keen intelligence. It seemed to him that with her swift feminine acumen she had found the ideal solution to the problem that confronted them.

'It's a thought,' he said. 'The only catch,' he went on, doubts beginning to creep in, 'is that they would find the thing gone, and it wouldn't be any too easy to explain on the spur of the moment why it wasn't there.'

Again Kelly felt that she was losing her grip on the scenario. His words left her with the impression that he was deliberately making things complicated.

'They?'

'The trustees.'

'Who are they?'

'I've forgotten. Some legal firm or other.'

'And they come nosing around?'

'I think they send a man down from time to time to see that everything is all right. I haven't been at this heirloom-possessing game long enough myself to be able to tell you definitely, but my friend Wade-Pigott, who has a friend who has a number of the beastly things, tells me that that's what they do. It seems plausible. They would naturally want to be sure there was no funny business going on.'

'Would this be at regular intervals?'

'I don't quite follow you.'

'I mean, do you get a letter from them saying their representative will call at two-thirty-five sharp a week from next Wednesday, or does the fellow look in just when he happens to feel like it?'

'The latter, I think.'

'So he might not be here for months.'

'I suppose not.'

'Then it's in the bag. When he does come and tells you the thing's gone and starts what-the-hell-ing, you simply slap your forehead and say "Good Lord, it must have been that guy Stickney". "Stickney?" says the fellow. "Man who was staying here coupla months ago," you say. "He must have swiped it. I remember now he told me he collected paperweights. Tut tut," you say, "I'd never have thought it of him. Such an honest face! Ah well, too late to do anything about it now", you say. And it will be too late, because by that time Wendell'll be back in the States and they won't be able to touch him. He'll be outside the jurisdiction or whatever they call it. I shouldn't be surprised if that sort of thing wasn't going on all the time all over England. Any questions?'

Henry had none. He was lost in admiration of her lucid reasoning. Wendell probably had several, but he was suffering from a temporary paralysis of his vocal cords. His emotions were mixed. On the one hand, his correct soul shivered austerely at the thought of lending his imprimatur to a scheme so directly in opposition to all he had been taught at his mother's knee. On the other hand, he wanted that paperweight, and

Kelly, say what you might of her code of ethics, had unquestionably sketched out a way of getting it.

'It would work,' said Henry, convinced.

'Sure it would work,' said Kelly. 'You've got a story no trustee could punch a hole in. It isn't as if you had to fake a burglary and notify the police and have them spot in a second that it wasn't on the level. The thing's in a glass case up there in the picture gallery that's not even locked. Wendell could have snitched it any time he pleased. I'll go and do it now, shall I? No time like the present.'

She hurried off, all girlish enthusiasm, and Wendell's vocal cords were at last able to function. It was plain that he had been following a train of thought.

'Paradene,' he said.

'Yes?' said Henry.

Wendell uttered a curious bronchial sound, half bleat and half gurgle.

'The people who buy heirlooms . . . do they go to prison?'

'They certainly do,' said Henry cheerily. 'Dartmoor's full of them.'

'Oh?' said Wendell.

Silence fell – on Wendell's part a moody one. It was broken by the return of Kelly. She was even cheerier than Henry.

'All set,' she announced. 'I've put it in with your socks and handkerchiefs in the chest of drawers in your bedroom, Wendell.'

'But somebody may find it!'

'Naturally I thought of that. You don't want to keep it laying there long. What I'd suggest is pack the old paperweight in a parcel and take it to the post office in the village and mail it to your bank in London. Wendell keeps an account in London,' she explained to Henry, 'so that if anything special comes along, he can just sign a cheque for it.'

'A very good idea,' said Henry. 'Don't you think it's a good idea, Stickney?'

'An excellent idea,' said Wendell, who had brightened considerably. He still found it impossible to regard his aunt's machinations with approval, but he could not deny that she got results.

'I thought you'd like it,' said Kelly. 'Do it now, right away. Then you won't have anything to worry about for the rest of the day.'

Behind them somebody coughed. It was a soft cough such as might have proceeded from a sheep troubled with asthma, but its effect on the three conspirators could hardly have been more pronounced if a lion had suddenly roared in their immediate rear. Henry quivered from stem to stern. Wendell sprang perhaps two inches into the air, and even Kelly seemed emotionally disturbed. Each spun sharply on his or her axis, and they were thus enabled to see that Clarkson was standing deferentially in the doorway.

'Pardon me, sir,' he said, addressing his remarks to Wendell, who was now back on terra firma. 'Might I have your permission to go to the village?'

Wendell seemed to swallow something hard and jagged. He spoke with difficulty.

'Yes. Yes. Of course. Certainly.'

'Thank you, sir,' said Clarkson, and went off to get the bowler hat without which no English valet stirs abroad. The rules of the Valets Guild are very strict on this point.

He left behind him a silence of the kind which some call tense and others pregnant. If he had been a messenger in a Greek play bringing bad news from the battle front, he could scarcely have created more consternation. Wendell had not ceased for an instant to quake in every limb. His voice emerged in a husky whisper.

'Do you think he heard?'

'No,' said Henry, always the optimist.

'He may have been standing there all the time we were talking.'

'Of course he wasn't,' said Kelly. 'Stop fussing, honey. Everything's all right. Come along and we'll hunt up a cardboard box and some brown paper and string, and I'll fix that parcel for you. Be sure to register it.'

4

In scouting the idea that Clarkson had overheard their business talk Henry and Kelly had been quite right. He had coughed immediately upon his entry on the scene, and all that had reached his ears had been the latter's statement that she thought they would like it. What they would like and why whatever it was would give them pleasure he did not know, nor did this ignorance worry him. His mind was concentrated exclusively on his own affairs.

Ever since the night of Kelly's interrupted trip to Coney Island, Clarkson had been giving serious consideration to the problem of what steps, if any, he should take with this sort of thing going on. Should he continue serving Wendell or should he resign his portfolio? It was not an easy decision to make, for his was a job that undeniably had many attractions. The pay was good and the duties extremely light. But could a man of his high principles go on polishing the shoes and pressing the trousers of an employer whose aunt was so intimately known to the police?

It was coming back to England that had turned the scale in favour of handing in his resignation. It had shown him where his career must lie. He did not dislike New York, but he realized now that he had never been able quite to adjust himself to life in a city where a tart was called a pie and the tea for his afternoon cuppa came in little cotton bags. It had required only a few days in his native land to convince him that the time had come for Mr Stickney and himself to part. He had written to the agency with which he dealt, informing them that he was now prepared to consider offers, and this morning a letter had arrived from them with details of an excellent situation which was at his disposal provided that he could let them know at once. Would he, they said, kindly telegraph, and it was with the object of kindly telegraphing that he was now on his way to the village.

The post office at Ashby Paradene, like so many rural post offices, combined its official duties with the selling of picture postcards, bilious-looking sweets, comic books for children and the like. It was presided over by an old lady of grim aspect who was inclined to be brusque with her clientele if her rheumatism had been troubling her, and it was unfortunate for Clarkson that it was giving her a good deal of discomfort just as he entered. She replied to his polite Good day with a frosty grunt, and was equally taciturn when he handed in his telegram. Only when she had counted the words did she speak, and then it was merely to state the small sum she required of him. And it was at this point that he discovered that even this was too much for him to disburse, for he had inadvertently left the wallet which contained all his funds on the table in his bedroom.

It was an annoying contretemps, but laughing lightly as a man will when he realizes that the joke is on him he explained the situation, adding that he was staying at Ashby Hall and asking if she would mind if he postponed payment until later. He soon received his answer. She did mind.

This came as a blow to Clarkson, placing him in the position of having to walk back to the Hall, walk back to the village and then walk back to the Hall again, a testing feat for one who had never gone in much for athletics. He pleaded that it was a most important telegram and one which must go off at once. Finding that this produced no softening in the iron features behind the wire entanglement, he heaved a sigh and was about to move away, when a voice behind him said 'Can I help?' and turning he saw a young man with a picture postcard in his hand. Reading from left to right, Bill Hardy.

Bill had come to the post office because on his return to the Beetle and Wedge he had found a telegram awaiting him. It was signed Algy, and it ran as follows:

COME BACK IMMEDIATELY AND WITHOUT FAIL. VITALLY IMPORTANT CONFER WITH YOURE SCHEME OF A LIFE-TIME. DROP EVERYTHING AND CATCH EARLIEST TRAIN. WIRE TIME OF ARRIVAL.

and it was his intention to expend a shilling or so telling Algy not to be an ass. He had seldom heard a suggestion as laughable as this of his old friend that he should absent himself from a locality where at any moment he might meet the other's sister Jane again and have another of those enthralling talks with her.

Arriving at the post office and finding the telegram window occupied by a man in a bowler hat, he had filled in the time of waiting by looking through the picture postcards on the other side of the shop, and among these he had found a coloured presentation of Ashby Hall. His initial emotion, like that of everybody who saw the Hall for the first time, was one of shock. In spite of Jane's warning he had not been prepared for anything quite so hideous. It had obviously been designed by an architect steeped to the tonsils in spirituous liquor, as so many architects were in the days of the Regency.

But hideous or not, it was the house where the girl he loved was living, and sentiment urged him to buy the card. It was cheap and it would fit neatly into the coat pocket next his heart. He had picked it up and was looking about for someone who would sell it to him, when he became aware that trouble of some sort had raised its head at the telegram window, and a moment's eavesdropping enabled him to gather what the trouble was.

It generally happens that the one thing a man who has fallen in love starts looking out for is an opportunity of doing some act of kindness to some fellow creature, and Bill was no exception to this rule. Since parting from Jane he had been filled with a sort of Boy Scoutful benevolence towards the whole human race. If a child had been present, he would have patted its head and bought it an ounce or two of the bilious-looking sweets, probably throwing in a couple of comic books for good measure. If a beggar had approached him and revealed himself as being short of funds, he would have sprung to the task of straightening out his financial difficulties. Neither of these outlets for his bounteousness being at the moment available, he was delighted that he had this bowler-hatted man to fall back on. The exchanges he had overheard had told him that the bowler-hatted one needed the price of a telegram, and nothing would give him greater pleasure than to bring him aid and comfort.

So he said 'Can I help?' and was assured by Clarkson that he could. Money changed hands, the old lady grudgingly accepted it, the telegram was dispatched, Bill handed in his own telegram and paid for the picture postcard, and Clarkson was at liberty to express his gratitude. He did this at some length, for he was deeply stirred, and it was as they stood there, their heads close together and Clarkson speaking urgently into Bill's left ear, that Wendell Stickney came in with his parcel.

It may be that the collecting of French eighteenth-century paperweights does something to a man's nervous system, unfitting him for a life of crime by robbing him of the coolness and calm which the criminal classes find so essential in the exercise of their profession, but whether this is so or not it is an undoubted fact that Wendell was completely lacking in the qualities that go to make a good crook. Where Henry had seemed unmoved by the dark deed they were undertaking and Kelly was plainly as nonchalant as a fish on ice, he had felt from the very inception of the scheme as if spiders to the number of several dozens were parading up and down his spinal cord. The only thing that enabled him to sustain his part in the enterprise was the thought of what a tone this treasure would lend to his collection in New York, if he succeeded in getting it there.

If! That was the operative word. What Henry had said with reference to the trustees' hirelings – private detectives he assumed they would be – who watched over heirlooms and swooped down at irregular intervals to make sure that they were still there had left him quaking with apprehension. Who could say that one of them was not even now in the neighbourhood, waiting to pounce? And what more than anything caused the spiders to quicken their steps and in some cases to form gangs and dance square dances on his sensitive skin was the thought of Clarkson.

Henry had dismissed lightly the possibility that Clarkson might have heard all, and Kelly had assured him that everything was all right, but he found it impossible to share their sunny outlook. Try as he would, he could not shake off the chilling conviction that Clarkson was in full possession of the facts and might quite conceivably at this very moment be pouring them into the receptive ear of one of the trustees' righthand men. The thought caused him to suffer such a sensation of bonelessness that he found a difficulty in opening the post office door. When he had managed to do so and was on the point of crossing the threshold, the first thing he saw was Clarkson in earnest conversation with a young man in a tweed coat and grey flannel trousers, who appeared to be drinking in the valet's every word with the most intense interest.

It was established earlier that people who encountered Bill for the first time were struck by his resemblance to a motion picture gangster. To Wendell he seemed to have all the earmarks of the tougher type of private detective, the very sort of private detective a board of trustees, anxious to secure the best, would have picked first from a long line of applicants. And there was Clarkson plainly bringing him up to date on conditions at Ashby Hall. There could be no other explanation of his garrulity. And in another moment he, Wendell, would have walked right up to them with the parcel in his hand – the parcel the nature of whose contents had no doubt just been made clear to the human bloodhound.

A strong shudder shook Wendell from his thinning hair to the soles of his shoes. The spiders were now doing one of those big production numbers so popular in revue, where the whole strength of the company let themselves go in uninhibited dance. He had the feeling he had sometimes had in nightmares that he was falling from a height into a black chasm.

Tottering backwards he regained the street. The Beetle and Wedge being so handy, he dragged himself through its doorway and into the saloon bar, where in a hoarse voice he ordered a double brandy. It was not his habit to drink so early in the day and far less to drink double brandies, but he recognized this as a special occasion.

And he had scarcely taken his first sip when the door opened and the detective in the grey flannel trousers came in, ordered a pint of mild and bitter and gave him a look so plainly one of dark suspicion that he rose like a rocketing pheasant and was off and away before Bill, who had been about to tell him it was a nice day, was able to get beyond the opening N of the word 'nice'.

Chapter Six

1

Henry's dinner party, like all dinner parties at which his friend Wade-Pigott was the host, had been a lengthy affair, and it was late when he returned to the Hall. He was feeling well-fed and happy and very appreciative of the beauty of the night. The air was fragrant with the scents of summer and a full moon cast black shadows on the terrace. He had reached the steps that led to it and was thinking that twenty years ago he would have slept out in the open on a night like this, when a voice from the darkness uttered the word 'Hi!' causing him to leap like a lamb in Springtime and lose the thread of his thoughts.

He had no difficulty in identifying the speaker. Only one member of the Hall circle would have opened the conversation with that monosyllable.

'Hullo, Kelly,' he said, speaking a little thickly, for he had bitten his tongue. 'What are you doing out here at this time of night?'

She came down the steps, and his heart gave a leap. Moonlight seldom fails to enhance a beautiful woman's beauty, and she had never looked so alluring. It suddenly flashed upon him with all the abruptness of a revelation that the restless feeling her society had been causing him these last days was love. It was an emotion he had experienced once or twice before in his youth, but then his fancy had generally turned to dumb blondes. Now middle-aged and capable of maturer judgement, he could see how vastly superior was the intelligent brunette, and of intelligence she had given ample evidence with her inspired suggestion in the matter of what to do with family heirlooms.

Yes, this, he recognized, making a swift diagnosis, was unquestionably love, and by one of those ironies of life of which

Thomas – not Bill – Hardy had been wont to write so feelingly he was debarred by poverty from pouring out his passion. A man with scruples and next to no income must be guarded in his speech and reserved in his deportment. He addressed himself to the difficult task of keeping the conversation on an unemotional level.

'I was waiting for you, Hank,' said Kelly. 'We've got to have a conference.'

'Something wrong?'

'Things aren't going quite according to plan. How was your dinner party?'

'Fine.'

'Hear any new ones?'

'They were new to me.'

'You must tell them to me some time. I'm always eager to add to my repertoire.'

'You shall have them. But you were saying things weren't going according to plan. What's the trouble?'

'Wendell's having conniption fits about that darned paperweight.'

'Why? He shipped it off all right, didn't he?'

'That's just what he didn't do.'

'But I thought he was going to.'

'That was the idea. But when he got to the post office, the first thing he saw was Clarkson yacking away to a sinister character who looked like a private eye, and he was sure he was dishing the dirt about that little business arrangement of ours. So he backed away and went to the inn for a bracer, and he hadn't been there a minute when in came the private eye and gave him a nasty piercing look as much as to say "What I know about *you*, Mac!" It scared the pants off him. Do those trustees of yours hire detectives to watch over the heirlooms?'

'Of course they don't.'

'How do you know?'

'Well, I don't actually know, but it doesn't seem likely.'

'Then who was the fellow Clarkson was talking to?'

'Just somebody he'd happened to get into conversation with, I suppose. Why shouldn't he talk to people in post offices? I've done it myself, often. I'm not worried about Clarkson. I don't think he could possibly have heard us.'

'Me neither. But try selling that idea to Wendell. You wouldn't get to first base.'

'He takes the gloomy view?'

'In spades. He's fired Clarkson.'

'You don't say?'

'Threw him out with his baggage and derby hat the moment he established contact.'

'Drastic.'

'And I'll bet he's regretting it now. He'll be sunk without Clarkson.'

This surprised Henry. He was quite fond of Mr Stickney and found much in him to respect, but he had never thought of him as one of those fastidious dressers who become spent forces if their valets leave them. The impression he had formed was that this guest of his clothed himself for comfort rather than display. The suits he favoured were not cut to give the wearer the appearance of perfect physical development but were merely designed to allow him plenty of room under the arms, and the same thing applied to his shirts. The only thing sartorially spectacular about him was his tie, which suggested – erroneously – that he was a member of the Brigade of Guards. It perplexed Henry that he should have needed the services of a valet at all.

Kelly was able to throw light on this mystery.

'You see, Wendell's rather peculiarly situated. You don't know his sister, do you? Mrs Loretta Stickney Pound? But of course you don't. Why should you? She's pure poison ivy,' said Kelly, summing up her niece by marriage with the pith and brevity so characteristic of her. 'She was the spearhead of the opposition when Theodore sprang it on the family that he and I were planning a merger. She's one of those strong-minded broads, and she's always had Wendell hypnotized. It started in their childhood days. She's three years older than him, and you know what that means when you're kids. She bossed him, and he's never gotten over it. She still orders him around, and instead of telling her to go soak her head he just says "Yes, ma'am" as weak as a newborn jellyfish and does what she tells him without letting out a yip. You get the picture?'

Henry got the picture.

'So when she told him that a man in his position has to have a valet, he didn't come back at her with a "Says who?" he just let her hire one for him, and that's how Clarkson came into the home.'

Henry tut-tutted sympathetically. So that was why Wendell Stickney always had that rather melancholy look. He had supposed it was due to not getting enough paperweights, but apparently what caused it was the strain of having a personal attendant. He had never had a personal attendant himself, except for dressers in the old days, but he could well imagine how Clarkson must have cast a gloom on Wendell Stickney's life.

'I suppose he hated it?' he said, and Kelly said No, this was not the case.

'They got along fine. There's a thing about Wendell you've probably missed. He may be a spineless worm when it comes to telling Loretta where to get off, but he has a sort of animal cunning that serves him well in an emergency. He told Clarkson he would double his wages if he just left him alone and didn't fuss over him. He could shine his shoes, he said, and he'd go so far as to allow him to press his pants now and then, but not a step further. You see, what he was afraid of was that Clarkson, having been raised on dukes and earls and all like that, would want to load him up with a whole lot of new suits, and Wendell likes to wear a suit till it looks like a tramp cyclist's second best. Well, Clarkson didn't object, and the deal went through. But you see what's happened now. Loretta'll get him another valet, and this one may not be as easy to make a gentleman's agreement with. So what I've got to do is find one who'll operate along Clarkson lines and sign him up before Loretta gets back.'

'Where is she now?'

'On a world cruise.'

'That'll hold her for awhile.'

'Yes.'

'So no need to worry for the moment.'

'That's true.'

'Especially as we've other things to worry about.'

'You said it. That paperweight sequence. What are your views on that?'

Henry pondered.

'Well, I suppose the best thing to do is to put it back in its glass case till this private eye, if he is a private eye, has blown over.'

'That's what I think, too, and that's what I told Wendell. But you can't pry him loose from the thing. He says if it's put back like you say, you'll change your mind and not let him have it.'

'And lose a thousand pounds? He's crazy.'

'Sure he is, but what can you expect of a man who collects paperweights? I put that to him, but he wouldn't budge. And he refuses to take it to the post office himself and mail it, on account he's scared the private eye will catch him with the goods on him. And he won't let you take it because he thinks that if you get your hands on it, you'll stick to it. So where do we go from here?'

'To bed, I suggest, and sleep on it. We'll probably think of something.'

'Maybe you're right. Kind of hot, though, for going indoors. How would you feel about a swim in the lake?'

'Not tonight, I think. Tomorrow, perhaps.'

'All right, then let's turn in.'

2

In her bedroom Kelly lit her last cigarette of the day and gave herself up to meditation. She was thinking how much she loved Henry and wishing, for her woman's instinct told her that he felt the same for her as she did for him, that he could bring himself to adopt the forthright methods of the late Theodore Stickney. She had spoken to Jane of Theodore kissing her like a ton of bricks, and it was precisely thus that she would have liked Henry to kiss her. His failure to do so, she supposed, was due to his being English. An Englishman, she thought bitterly, would have to have a signed permit from a girl before he felt justified in kissing her.

She crushed out her cigarette and went to bed, and it was as she did so that Bill, who for some twenty minutes had been standing in the shadow of a tree, decided that it was about time to return to the Beetle and Wedge and crossed the lawn with that object in view. He had come to the Hall rather in the spirit of a devotee visiting a shrine. It was where Jane lived, and for a man in love to go and gaze at the home of the girl he loves, particularly by moonlight, is practically routine. But even a man in love has got to get his sleep, so after pausing for one last look he reluctantly went on his way.

He had scarcely gone when there was a shaky tap at Kelly's door, and Wendell appeared. In addition to striped pyjamas and a purple dressing gown he was wearing a look of extreme agitation.

'Did I wake you?' he said.

'No, I wasn't asleep. Want to borrow an aspirin or something?'

Wendell was looking as if he could have done with several.

'Aunt Kelly,' he said, 'that man is here!'

'What man?'

'The man Clarkson was talking to in the post office, he is prowling on the lawn. I saw him from my window.'

'You must have imagined it. What would he be prowling on lawns for? It was probably an owl.'

Wendell did not actually dance with annoyance, but he gave the impression that he would have done so if he could have remembered the steps.

'It was not an owl! I saw his face clearly in the moonlight.'

'You're not kidding?'

'Certainly not.'

'It really was this guy?'

'I could not have been mistaken. He was standing on the lawn, and ... Where are you going?'

'Out,' said Kelly briefly. 'It's about time we had a showdown with that character. If he likes to give you nasty looks in saloon bars, that's his privilege, I guess, but if he thinks he can come prowling on private lawns as if he owned them I'm going to see that he thinks again. It isn't as if there was a sign out saying "Basket parties welcome". Gimme that poker.'

'Please be careful.'

'Don't worry about me. He's the one that's in line for a cauliflower ear.'

3

Nine o'clock next morning found Henry at the breakfast table brooding over the letters that had come by the early post. They were not having a cheering effect. One in particular had damped his spirits. It was from the firm of Duff and Trotter informing him that as they had received no reply to their communications asking for a settlement of his account, they would be reluctantly compelled to take steps. He was speculating moodily as to the precise meaning those eminent merchants of fine foods and wines attached to the word 'steps' – surely they would not go to the lengths they had gone with Algy – when Kelly entered.

'Morning, Hank.'

'Good morning, Kelly.'

'You look worried. Something wrong?'

There are subjects on which a man has to be secretive. Henry loved this woman, but even to her he was not prepared to reveal the vultures which were gnawing at his bosom.

'Just some annoying letters,' he said. 'You aren't looking very bright yourself.'

'No, I'm worried, too. Have you a ghost in this joint?'

'Not that I know of. Why?'

'Wendell came to me last night after I left you, all worked up. Said he'd seen a man on the lawn. And not just *a* man, *the* man. The one who gives him dirty looks in saloon bars. I went out with a poker to investigate, and of course there was no one there. I had the idea it might have been the Paradene spectre, but if you say there isn't one, it must mean that Wendell's cracking under the strain and beginning to see things.'

'That's bad.'

'Couldn't be worse. When they start doing that, you're in trouble. Theodore used to see things from time to time, so it looks as if it kind of runs in the family. Do you know what I believe is wrong with him?'

'What's that?'

'Having got rid of Clarkson and realizing that he's left the door wide open for Loretta to put in her nominee, he's in some sort of shock. I'm going to London today and get him a valet before she can do anything. I'll take an evening train and stay at a hotel for the night, so that I can see a show. You wouldn't care to come along?'

'I'd love to, but I promised to talk to the vicar about the school treat.'

'Stand him up.'

'I've done that twice. I can't do it again.'

'A pity. It would have been fun going on the town together. Still, that's life. But about Wendell. It's too bad all this had to happen to spoil his visit. He was enjoying it here so much. He's crazy about this place.'

Henry started.

'About the Hall?'

'Sure. He told me so. He said how wonderful it was to think of all his ancestors living here for hundreds of years. You wouldn't think it, but he's very romantic.'

Henry was wondering if this was not too good to be true.

'He really likes this architectural abortion?'

'It's his dream house.'

'Then I wish he'd buy it.'

Kelly was astounded.

'You wouldn't sell?'

'Wouldn't I!'

'But I thought you landed proprietors, if that's what you call them, would rather die than part with the old home.'

'Not this landed proprietor. What I want is money.'

'Don't we all?'

'And I'll tell you why. If I had a nice big chunk of money, I would ask you to marry me.'

'What!'

'You heard.'

'Why, Hank Paradene, you could knock me down with a lipstick! You really want to team up with me?'

'More than anything on earth.'

'Well, what an extraordinary coincidence. I was thinking only last night, when we were chatting in the moonlight, that the one thing that would make my day would be teaming up with *you.*'

It is difficult for a man seated at a breakfast table to leap to his feet, but by sending his chair flying across the room Henry contrived to do so.

'Kelly!'

'I've been that way about you since the first day we met.'

'I can't believe it!'

'What strikes you as odd?'

'You're so wonderful.'

'Well, so are you.'

'Me? I'm nothing. I'm a sort of elderly Algy.'

'Who's Algy?'

'My nephew. He's a loafer, and so am I. I'm not worthy to kiss the whatever-it-is of your garment.'

'If that's all you want to kiss,' said Kelly. 'Now there's a thing that should be done every hour on the hour, if not oftener,' she added after an interval had passed.

Henry was still dubious.

'Are you sure you aren't making a mistake?'

'Sure I'm sure.'

'If Stickney doesn't buy the house we'll be frightfully hard up.'

'What of it?'

'You won't mind?'

'I'll enjoy it. I always think that people who marry on practically nothing have a swell time. If you're poor, you enjoy whooping it up when you can manage it. If you're rich, you just get bored with pleasure and probably drift apart.'

Henry could not follow her there. Loth as he was to disagree with her lightest word, this was going too far.

'No,' he said firmly, 'if I had a million I wouldn't drift apart from you.'

'You might.'

'I wouldn't.'

'I'm only saying you might.'

'But I shouldn't.'

'Well, anyway,' said Kelly, yielding the point, 'all I'm saying is that it'll be much more fun having to watch the budget and going up to London for lunch and a matinée if like it was my birthday or your birthday or something, and me making my own clothes than – than –'

'Not.'

'Yes, than not. It would have spoiled everything if Theodore had left me a million instead of passing on with enough debts to choke a horse.'

'You're absolutely right. We should have missed all the fun we're going to have, and we shouldn't have felt so close together.'

'Exactly. Do you know, I knew a wretched young slob over in New York who came into about twenty million when his father died, and he went and married a girl with double that.'

'What became of him?' asked Henry, shocked.

'I don't know. We lost touch. But just imagine that marriage!'

'Awful!'

'What possible fun could they have had?'

'It doesn't bear thinking of. What was his name?'

'Cadwallader. And hers was Allenby.'

For some moments, deeply affected by the tragedy of these two poor bits of human wreckage, they stood in silence. Henry felt near to tears, and he thought Kelly was bearing up only with difficulty. She was the first to speak.

'What's under that dish?' she said.

'Kippered herrings,' said Henry.

'Lead me to them,' said Kelly. 'I could eat a dozen.'

Chapter Seven

1

The train from London paused at Ashby Paradene to discharge passengers, and from it there emerged two small boys, two small girls, a curate, three farmers, a retired Colonel and Algy Martyn. He had come at considerable expense – only the pawning of his cuff-links had made the journey possible – to reproach his friend Bill Hardy. He was extremely annoyed with Bill, and did not intend to mince his words.

Everything in Ashby Paradene was near everything else, and not more than a few steps separated the station from the Beetle and Wedge. Algy covered the distance in quick time and a few minutes after he had given up his ticket he was in the lounge, gazing sternly at Bill.

'I got your telegram,' he said in a low, cold voice.

'I thought you would,' said Bill. 'I was betting on it.'

'And I don't mind telling you it came as a pretty severe shock. It isn't pleasant for a man who has a cast-iron scheme on the fire and needs only a friend's sympathy and co-operation to steer it to success to be fobbed off with a flippant instruction not to be an ass. How do you suppose John D. Rockefeller, when he was trying to raise capital to start Standard Oil, would have felt if people had told him not to be an ass?'

Bill pointed out that all this embarrassment could have been avoided if Algy had refrained from being an ass, but added, for he was a fair-minded man, that this was perhaps too much to expect.

'You and your cast-iron schemes!'

'Do you want to hear about this one?'

'No.'

'It runs as follows. Are you by any chance acquainted with

a wayside inn called The Green Man in Rosendale Road, Valley Fields?'

'No.'

'Nice little pub,' said Algy approvingly. 'Good beer, and they give you credit, which is the vital thing. I was in there yesterday, and I met a man who has a house in Croxley Road. I got into conversation with him – in the hope, I confess, of getting him to buy me a drink, which I am happy to say he eventually did, though not before hints had been dropped. Yes, I dare say you do think this is the dullest story you ever heard, but keep listening, because the plot is about to thicken. I got into conversation with this bloke, as I say, and I found him in peevish mood. It seemed that he was an old inhabitant and it was his opinion that all these building operations that were going on in its midst were turning Valley Fields from a peaceful rural retreat into a sort of suburban Manchester. He said he was thankful that he was clearing out. Mark that, Bill. He said he was clearing out. "Oh?" I said. "Clearing out, are you?" and he said the firm he works for was sending him to Rio de Janeiro and he was sailing almost immediately. Fortunately, he said, he would be able to sell his house, because some syndicate or association or whatever you call those concerns wanted to build a block of flats in Croxley Road and his residence came right in the middle of the chunk of land they were planning to do it on. He told me they were offering him eight thousand quid. I instantly told him I would give him ten.'

Throughout this long and totally uninteresting narrative Bill had been doing his best not to listen, but it had not been easy to avoid catching some of it, and these last words arrested his attention in no uncertain manner.

'You *what*!'

'I said I would give him ten. That's how you win to ease and affluence, Bill, by thinking like lightning and being right there to open the door when opportunity knocks. You will of course have spotted what I had in mind. These building bounders have to have that house or they can't go ahead with their flat project, so whoever owns it is in a position to do a bit of bargaining. The Croxley Road man, having to sail for Peru or wherever Rio de Janeiro is almost immediately, isn't able to sit tight and haggle. I, on the other hand, am, and I have tentatively fixed twenty thousand as the asking price. So to cut a long story short we reached an agreement there and then and drew it up on the back of an old envelope I happened to have with me, and the landlord of the pub and the pot-boy – nice fellow, his name's Erbut, you must meet him some time – did the witnessing. I am to pay the householder five hundred pounds a week from now and give him an I.O.U. for the rest, and the house is mine. So when I sell it for twenty thousand I shall have a nice profit of ten, and with a capital of ten thousand there is no estimating where I shall finish. It's that first solid chunk of money in the bank that gets you going. The inventive brain does all the rest. So there's my cast-iron scheme. See any flaws in it?'

Bill was at length able to speak, though with difficulty.

'Just one.'

'Which is?'

'Where are you going to get the five hundred?'

Algy's eyebrows rose. He had expected that his old friend would have been quicker on the uptake than this.

'From you, of course, Bill, old man. Naturally I'll pay you liberal interest.'

'You won't have to pay any interest.'

Algy was plainly touched. He said that that was just like Bill, generous to a fault. It was men of Bill's stamp, he added, who gave one some hope for the human race.

'But I must insist that we keep this on a business basis. If you're lending me five hundred pounds, you are entitled to at least five per cent on your money, and I won't put up a fight if you make it ten.'

'I'm not lending you five hundred pounds.'

Algy seemed stunned. He stared incredulously.

'Are you telling me you refuse? Has it slipped your memory that we were at school together and that when there I frequently shared with you my last pot of strawberry jam, not to mention letting you in on the anchovy paste I could ill

92

spare? I should have thought the most ordinary gratitude –'

'It isn't a question of refusing. I haven't got it.'

'Come, come, Bill. Eight hundred a year you told me you were getting. That means your capital must be around twenty thousand.'

'It is, but I can't touch it.'

Algy's jaw dropped like a tired lily.

'You can't? Why not?'

'It's in trust. I get the interest, but I can't touch the capital.'

'Who says so?'

'The will says so.'

'You're sure?'

'Pretty sure.'

'Well, this opens up a new line of thought,' said Algy.

His distress was so manifest that Bill's kindly heart was stirred.

'I'll tell you what I'll do, if you like. I'll go to London and see my lawyer, just in case I'm wrong. There's a train in about an hour.'

'Do that, Bill,' said Algy, hope instantly reviving. 'I'm convinced that you've got the whole thing muddled up, no doubt because you allowed your mind to wander when the legal eagle was doing his stuff. It's always impossible to listen to a lawyer droning on about whereases and heretofors and all that without your attention floating off to other things. You must have misunderstood him. It stands to reason that a testator wouldn't be such a dope as to leave a fellow a wad of money and stick in a clause saying that he wasn't allowed to spend it. I mean,' said Algy, reasoning closely, 'testators may be asses, but they're not silly asses.'

2

Up at the Hall while this business talk was in progress at the Beetle and Wedge, Jane, who had been seeing Mrs Simmons, the cook, about dinner, came out on to the terrace and sat down in pensive mood. She was trying to make her mind up about Lionel Green.

Although in the days that had passed since their meeting at the club her fury had cooled a good deal and she no longer wished that she could hit him with a brick, she had begun to wonder more and more if it would not be a move too far in the opposite direction to marry him.

Her interview with Mrs Simmons had done nothing to dispel her uneasiness. She had gone to the kitchen with the sole intention of talking about joints of beef, and how this topic had led into a monologue by her employee on the untrustworthiness of good-looking men she was unable to recall.

Most people seeing Mrs Simmons would have written her off as a woman unlikely to have her affections trifled with by the Adonis type of man, for her strong point was not allure. What she specialized in was cooking, not sex appeal. Nevertheless, she had had her romance and it had terminated abruptly in the departure of her suitor, who, as she put it, had legged it one morning without so much as saying goodbye.

Jane had been properly sympathetic, but her thoughts as she sat on the terrace were not of the Simmons tragedy but of her own dilemma. She was remembering what her brother Algernon had said to her on learning of her engagement. Prefacing his remarks with the statement that he had been at school with Lionel Green and so knew what he was talking about, he had told her in his brotherly way that she had the limited intelligence of a retarded rabbit. Lionel Green, he said, though admittedly a feast for the eye, was basically a louse, and she would never have dreamed of teaming up with him if she had not allowed herself to be dazzled by his sickening good looks. And she was asking herself now if Algy, though expressing himself crudely, might not have been right.

What she needed, she felt, was a wise counsellor who would tell her what to do for the best. Dorothy Dix would have been just right and so would Dear Abby, but neither unfortunately was available. To whom could she turn? And at this moment, as if he had read her thoughts, Henry came out of the house and she marvelled that it had not occurred to her to think of him. Elderly, kind and experienced, he filled precisely all her requirements.

Had she been less preoccupied, she would have noted a subtle change in Henry's demeanour since she had last seen him. Usually placid, he now gave the impression that pent-up emotions were effervescing within him and that it would not require a great deal of encouragement to make him skip like the high hills. His happiness was almost tangible.

Only one thing kept it from being perfect. Kelly, feeling perhaps rightly that in Wendell's agitated state of mind any added excitement might have the worst effects, upsetting his mental balance completely, had made him promise that their engagement should not for the present be announced. He was consequently unable to take Jane into his confidence, much though he would have liked to do so. There was, however, as far as he could see, no objection to his beaming at her, so he beamed.

'Hullo, Jane,' he said. 'What a wonderful day, Jane. Do you realize, Jane, that it's nearly a week since we've had a drop of rain? I can't remember when I've known that to happen in England. The papers keep whining that the crops need some, but I say To hell with the crops, let 'em Eat cake. I like it.'

'Henry,' said Jane, 'I'm worried.'

The idea of anyone being worried on this day of days appalled Henry. He sat down beside her and took her hand in his, all sympathy and concern. Dorothy Dix could not have been more anxious to soothe. Nor could Dear Abby.

'Good heavens!' he said. 'What's wrong?'

'I'm not sure anything is, but I'd like to have your advice. It's about Lionel.'

'You're thinking of that lunch?'

'Yes.'

It was impossible for Henry in his exalted mood not to look on the bright side. He agreed with her that Lionel's behaviour on that occasion had certainly been open to criticism, but he was sure that there must be some perfectly good explanation.

'Tarvin's really the boss of that concern of his, isn't he?'

'Yes, Lionel's only the junior partner.'

'So if Tarvin asked him to bring him along, it was probably difficult for him to refuse.'

'Then why didn't he tell me that? He had plenty of time to explain while we were waiting in the hall.'

'Would you say plenty of time? It seems to me that it required a longish explanation. In his place I'd have had to marshal my thoughts quite a bit. I'll tell you what to do,' said Henry, inspired. 'Ring him up now and ask him to give you lunch. Then you can talk the whole thing out comfortably. If you start for the station in twenty minutes or so, you can catch the 11.15.'

A wave of gratitude submerged Jane.

'Henry, you're an angel,' she said. 'I'll go and phone him now.'

The 11.15 was the train Bill was taking. They met on the platform.

3

It seemed to Bill, as they took their seats and the train began to gather speed, that one had here a striking illustration of how Providence always sees to it that the man who is doing a good deed shall have his reward. He had not had the slightest desire to go to London on a morning which, already warm and sticky, was plainly about to become warmer and stickier as the day wore on. He was going, at considerable personal discomfort, simply to oblige Algy, knowing perfectly well that he was merely wasting his time. His lawyer had made the conditions of his legacy clear to the meanest intelligence, and it was futile to travel all the way to London just to hear him repeat his remarks. But purely in order to bring a momentary gleam of sunshine into Algy's life he had undertaken the tedious expedition, and his kindness and unselfishness had not gone unnoticed in official circles. Here he was in a cosy railway compartment with Jane sitting opposite him and a journey of at least an hour and a quarter in prospect. There was certainly nothing niggardly in the way these things were handled by those in charge, when the case was sufficiently deserving.

Jane on her part had no complaints to make. If her ecstasy

fell somewhat short of the heights reached by his, she was glad to have his company and looked forward to a pleasant and entertaining tête-à-tête. Their previous meetings had left her with a great liking for this very agreeable young man with whom her relations had been from the start so comfortable and easy. Odd, she reflected, that they should have got along together from the first like a couple of twin souls, for she was not a girl readily attracted by strangers. Odd, too, that she should feel such curiosity about him, such an urge to have him tell her all about himself. She moved in a circle where the slightest word of encouragement was enough to extract from every man she met the story of a life, and as a rule her primary impulse when encountering males of the species was to check this tendency in them to become autobiographical. And yet the train had not travelled half a mile before she was saying 'Tell me –', and as at the same moment Bill said 'Algy –', there was a pause.

'I'm sorry,' said Bill. 'You were saying –'

'No, do go on. What about Algy?'

'Oh, nothing, really. I was only going to say that he turned up this morning.'

'What, here?'

'He's joined me at the inn.'

'You paying all expenses, no doubt?'

'Well, yes, I suppose so.'

'Quoth the raven!'

'Eh?'

'Private joke. My uncle always insists that the ravens feed Algy as they did what's-his-name in the Old Testament. You seem to be a raven in good standing.'

'Oh well, I can't let him starve.'

'Why not? Do him a world of good. Of course, the only real solution for Algy is marriage. He ought to marry some nice girl with a private income and an iron will, who would get behind him with a spiked stick and make him do a job of work.'

'Somebody like Lady Macbeth?'

'Lady Macbeth would be just right.'

'I'll suggest it to him when I get back. But what was it you were going to say?'

'When?'

'Before we got on to the subject of Algy you said "Tell me –" '

'Oh that? I was starting to say Tell me about yourself.'

'I'd much rather hear about you. I mean, all I know about you is that you're Algy's sister.'

'That's about all there is to know. I'm a very ordinary sort of person.'

'Ordinary!' said Bill, speaking with something of the shocked horror of a vicar whom one of his choir boys has surprised with a sudden expletive.

'I don't know what else you would call me. I'm just one of the working girls whom Heaven, according to a friend of mine, is said to protect. Born in London, educated at Cheltenham, working on a weekly paper. Hobbies, golf and tennis when I can get any and trying to galvanize Algy into earning an honest living. Nobody's going to get rich writing my biography. How about you? All I know so far is that you're good at getting cats down from trees, and there must be other sides to your character. School? I know where you went to school, because Algy said you were at his. What happened after that? Oxford? Cambridge?'

'Neither, worse luck. My uncle didn't approve of Universities. He was one of those men who go into business at the age of sixteen and think anything else is a waste of time.'

'But what had it got to do with him? How did he get into the act?'

'He was my guardian. My people died when I was about eight.'

'And he said you'd got to go into his business?'

'Yes. Import and export, if that means anything to you.'

'It doesn't.'

'It didn't mean much to me, and I wasn't eager to learn more. But this can't be interesting you.'

'Of course it is,' said Jane, and was surprised to realize how much it did. 'I'm drinking in every word. So what then?'

'I said I wouldn't.'

'Good for you. I don't suppose it went very well, did it?'

'Not very.'

'Did he disown you?'

'It amounts to that.'

'And you ran away to sea?'

'It sounds pretty conventional, but that is what I did.'

'Sailor before the mast?'

'I didn't rise quite as high as that in the social scale. I worked in the galley, assisting the cook.'

'And after that?'

'I had various jobs.'

'Such as?'

'Well, there were quite a number of them. Picking lemons, for one.'

'I knew it! The moment I saw you, I said to myself "That man has been picking lemons". Where was this?'

'Chula Vista, California.'

'Are there lemons out there?'

'Several.'

'And you climbed trees and picked them? That's where you got your cat technique, I suppose. Did you enjoy it?'

'Not much.'

'Still, better than exporting and importing, I should imagine.'

'Oh, yes. Very healthy life. But I wasn't sorry to give it up.'

'For what?'

'Oh, a series of jobs.'

A thought struck Jane.

'Have you ever told this saga of yours to Algy?'

'I did once.'

'Did your example shame him?'

'Not in the least. He said the mere idea of working like that made him sick, and my story confirmed the view he had always held that I ought not to be allowed at large.'

'Somebody ought to do something about that brother of mine,' said Jane, revolted. 'Were these jobs all in California?'

'All but the last one. I finally saved enough to get me to

New York, where I had my first real break. I got taken on as a sort of general assistant by a man who ran a Muldoon place on Long Island.'

'What on earth is a Muldoon place?'

'A health resort for tired business men. The first one was started years ago by a man named Muldoon, and there are lots of them now all over America. Simple living, fresh air and exercise. My job was to box with the customers and go riding with them and so on. I loved it.'

'So you can box?'

'A little. As a matter of fact, I suppose I'm really a pro, because I won twenty-five dollars for fighting a fellow in Chula Vista, the representative of a rival firm of lemon-pickers. It was the foundation of my fortunes. That was how I managed to get to New York and be taken on by the Muldoon man.'

Jane was looking at him with a good deal of respect. She admired men who did things, and in her sheltered life she met mainly those who talked at considerable length of the things they were going to do when they got around to it. She gave a sudden laugh.

'I was just thinking of Algy fighting fellows in Chula Vista for twenty-five dollars,' she said in answer to Bill's look of inquiry.

Or, she thought disloyally, Lionel Green.

'Why aren't you still with the Muldoon man?' she asked.

'He had domestic trouble. He didn't actually tell me so, but I think he had a number of ex-wives, all demanding alimony, so he felt the best way of cutting down expenses was to come to England and start a similar establishment here. He did, and is doing very well. He took me with him. I was working for him more than two years. In Hampshire, near Portsmouth.'

'Still loving it?'

'Yes. It was a wonderful life. And then I let my uncle talk me into going into his business.'

'But I thought you weren't speaking to each other.'

'So did I. But I happened to run into him one afternoon when I was taking my day off in London and we got quite friendly again. I told him what I was doing, and he said that sort of thing didn't lead anywhere, which I suppose was right, and he seemed so anxious for me to come back to him that I hadn't the heart to refuse. So there I was, stuck with an office job which I hated. It went on for a year or two, and then he died and left me this money.'

'And now you're going to live in the country and turn out spine-chillers. Got any ideas?'

'I'm full of them.'

'Then you're all right.'

'All right so far.'

'Self-employed and dealing in a product, as they say on What's My Line. I don't see how you can go wrong.'

'Well, anyway, I shall be living in the country.'

'Yes. I envy you. I wish I could. But I'm afraid I shan't be able to. The man I'm marrying is a partner in an antique shop, and that'll keep him tied to London, worse luck.'

4

The afternoon was well advanced by the time Bill returned from London. When he did so, there was that in his demeanour which would have reminded students of history of Napoleon after his experiences in Moscow. He was no stranger to the slings and arrows of outrageous fortune and as a rule was able to bear them stoically, but those frightful words which Jane had spoken as the train was drawing into Victoria had pierced his armour. As he entered the Beetle and Wedge, he was weighed down with a gloom which the sight of Algy restoring his tissues in the lounge with a whisky and soda did nothing to alleviate. There are moments in a man's life when encountering an old school friend tends to nauseate rather than cheer.

Algy, on the other hand, was plainly in considerably better spirits than he had been at their last meeting. In the course of the afternoon an idea had occurred to him which had done much to remove the furrows from his brow. It had shown him that even if Bill's lawyer had no balm to offer, all was not lost. It was with quite a rollicking wave of the hand that he greeted Bill and asked what the verdict was.

This was no time for slow and delicate breakings of bad news even if Bill had been in the mood for them.

'I was right,' he said. 'I'm not allowed to touch the capital.'

Algy nodded. He said he had feared as much.

'No getting round Clause Eighteen Sub-section Twelve, eh? Too bad. Well, it's nice of you to look so crushed about it and I appreciate your silent sympathy. But you will be relieved to hear that the blow, though shrewd, has not flattened me, partly because I was expecting it and partly because I've been thinking things over and have come up with what I feel is an inspiration calculated to straighten out my path and bring about the happy ending. What at first had all the earmarks of an impasse proves on investigation to be merely a momentary check. I see now that all I need is a rich man with a good business head who will be delighted to advance me money for a venture bound to result in quick and substantial profits, and it shouldn't be difficult to find one. You have been working in the City for quite a time. You must know dozens. Give me a few names and addresses.'

All this talk and chatter was weighing heavily on a man who wanted to be alone with his dark thoughts, but Bill was too amiable to refrain from doing his best to oblige a friend in need. He had no acquaintance, he said, with London's financiers, but suggested that Algy should try his uncle, and the next few moments were occupied by Algy in coughing, for he had imprudently laughed heartily while swallowing whisky and soda.

'Henry?' he gasped when he had recovered. 'He's nearly as broke as I am. Think again.'

Bill thought again. Like all lovers, he had total recall where the loved one's utterances were concerned, and there came back to him what Jane had said when buying chocolate bars.

'There's an American millionaire staying with your uncle.'

Algy sat up with a jerk. The Biblical horse that said 'Ha, ha' among the trumpets could not have displayed more animation.

'There is?'

'A man named Stickney.'

'Who told you that?'

'Your sister.'

'So you've met the young half-portion?' said Algy, interested. 'Since you came down here, I mean.'

'Yes, I've met her.'

'And she told you – officially – that this millionaire is on tap. Then he's my man. I must meet him and soften him up till he bears fruit. Heaven send that Henry hasn't already touched him for all he can spare. But a snag raises its ugly head. For some distorted reasons of his own Henry won't let me into the house, so you must be the one established there. Here is the procedure as I see it. I get hold of Jane and tell her to invite you to come and stay. Once in, you fraternize with this Stickney and get him to accompany you to the inn for a drink. I am waiting in readiness, crouched for the spring. You introduce me, and I do the rest. It can't fail. I'll get Jane on the phone right away.'

'No!'

'Did you say No?'

'Yes.'

'Oh, yes? I thought you said No!'

'I did. I'm not going near the Hall.'

'Why not?'

'Because I don't want to.'

'Why don't you want to?'

'Because,' said Bill, goaded into abandoning all reticence, 'I couldn't stand being with Jane ... hearing her voice ...'

This surprised Algy. Much of his time since their childhood had been spent in keeping his sister in her place and seeing to it that she did not get above herself, as a brother should, but he had never supposed that she was unattractive. Even when calling her a squirt and a half-portion he had thought of her as a comely squirt and a half-portion with plenty of sex appeal.

'I don't follow you,' he said. 'What's the matter with her voice? Sounds all right to me. Don't you like her?'

'Of course I like her.'

'And yet you're all for shunning her. I don't get it. Your mental processes ... Stap my vitals,' said Algy, struck with a sudden bizarre idea. 'Are you in love with her?'

'Yes,' said Bill, 'and she's engaged to someone else. So now you know why I won't go to the Hall.'

Algy frowned thoughtfully. He could see that the situation was one that called for all that he had of eloquence and persuasiveness. The first thing to do, of course, was to make it clear to his stricken friend that there was nothing final or irrevocable about his sister's unfortunate entanglement.

'Engaged to someone else, yes,' he conceded. 'But only to Lionel Green,' and when Bill said that he didn't see what the name of the man she was going to marry mattered, the salient fact being that she was going to marry him, he replied that that on the contrary was the whole nub and gist, because it was out of the question that any girl, however much she might in a moment of temporary insanity have got betrothed to him, would think seriously of marrying Lionel Green. The madness was bound to pass, leaving her once more in circulation. Good heavens, he said, driving home his point, hadn't Bill ever heard of girls breaking engagements?

Bill showed no sign of sharing his optimistic outlook.

'What makes you think she would want to break her engagement?' he asked, and Algy clicked his tongue impatiently. Nothing is more irritating than being forced by the slowness of one's auditor to repeat one's arguments.

'I told you. She's engaged to Lionel Green.'

Bill, too, seemed impatient.

'Who is this Lionel Green? You talk as if the name meant something to me.'

'Well, doesn't it?'

'Not a thing. What's wrong with the man? Is he a leper?'

'For all practical purposes. He's an interior decorator and sells antique furniture. And we always knew, did we not, that he would end up in some such way. We had him taped from the start. Ha!' cried Algy, enlightened. 'I see where we've gone astray. I have been speaking of him as Lionel Green and naturally the name didn't register. I should have said L. P. Green. You can't have forgotten L. P. Green. Throw your mind back. The old school. L. P. Green.'

'Oh!' said Bill.

He spoke dully. Memory had returned. L. P. Green was taking shape before his mental eye, and the spectacle did nothing to raise his spirits. It was the spectacle of a youth whose slender frame and delicately chiselled, if spotty, features made it inevitable that he would grow up to be just the sort of man to ensnare the female heart. Always assuming, of course, that since his school days the spots had yielded to treatment, as no doubt they had. It was perfectly absurd for Algy to babble about broken engagements. A girl betrothed to a despotted L. P. Green would not lightly give up such a prize. Spiritually, if he was anything like what he had been at the old Alma Mater, he might fall short of the ideal, but what would that weigh against his physical charms?

He rose abruptly.

'I'm going upstairs to have a bath,' he said, to the disappointment of Algy, who had been hoping for a long and invigorating talk about L. P. Green.

Chapter Eight

1

Jane had had a stroke of luck. Two strokes actually, one big, the other small. The small one was that she had got a lift home in a car, thus avoiding a stuffy railway journey. The other had to do with Lionel Green. As the net result of both, she returned to Ashby Hall with the conviction that things were breaking well for her.

The owner of the car was her colleague the book reviewer, the one who gave her novels of suspense. She had met him as she was on her way to the station to catch her train, and he, learning that she was bound for Ashby Paradene, had told her to hop in, as he was off to Brighton and Ashby Paradene was on the way. He dropped her at the great gates, and as she walked up the drive the feeling she had had all the afternoon that all was right with the world deepened. She approved of everything it had to offer. The sun was shining, and she liked the way it shone. The sky was blue, and she would not have had it otherwise. A rabbit, popping out of a bush, sat drinking her in with the pop-eyed stare habitual with rabbits all the world over, and it seemed to her the most attractive rabbit she had ever met. Even Ashby Hall, when she came in sight of it, lost eighty-five per cent of its hideousness and for the first time took on a certain weird beauty. Only a very little encouragement would have been needed to make her burst into song.

Henry was sitting in his favourite chair on the lawn, and she made for him on winged feet. He was just the man she wanted to see. She had news for him.

'Henry,' she said, 'do you want to hear a long and very funny story?'

He gave the question the drowsy consideration of a man

abruptly roused from slumber. Soothed by the warmth of the day, he had dropped off for a moment.

'If it's not too long. I'm expecting the vicar.'

'Well, I'll try to keep it short, but I don't want to leave out any of the good bits. It really is a scream from start to finish.'

'If it's the one about the clergyman's wife and the drunken sailor, Wade-Pigott told it to me last night.'

'No, it's not that one. They aren't telling it on the Stock Exchange yet. It's about Lionel. You remember I took your advice and rang up Lionel and asked him to give me lunch.'

'My memory's not so dulled with age that I can't recall that. How was it?'

'The lunch? I didn't get it. I had a bun and a cup of coffee at a tea shop.'

'Lover's quarrel?'

'Not exactly.'

'Then what?'

'This is where it starts to get funny. When I got to his revolting club, he wasn't there.'

Henry blinked, removing the last vestiges of sleep. His interest had been enchained.

'Not there?'

'No.'

'After arranging to meet you?'

'Yes, after arranging to meet me.'

'Is the man off his head?'

'Far from it, as you'll see if you'll stop interrupting me and let me get on with it. He wasn't there, but he had put on an understudy, his partner Orlo Tarvin. You remember him? The man behind the beard.'

'Was he ill?'

'Tarvin?'

'Lionel.'

'Oh, Lionel? No, I didn't gather so. Fit as a fiddle, as far as I know.'

'Then why wasn't he there?'

'That's the whole point of my story, and I see it isn't going to be such a long one after all. You know he went to America to decorate some millionaire's house. Well, in the course of his decorating he appears to have got engaged to the millionaire's daughter, and he had asked Tarvin to break the news to me. I suppose he didn't feel up to doing it himself.'

A good many people beside Algy had said derogatory things about L. P. Green in their time, but few of their strictures can have been so forceful as those of Henry on hearing this news item. He had spoken for perhaps half a minute before Jane was able to resume her story.

'Tarvin was very kind. He spent ages trying to console me, and I hadn't the heart to tell him that nothing could have pleased me more.'

Henry stared.

'Pleased you?'

'Delighted and relieved me. I'd gone there meaning to take Algy's advice and break the engagement over the after-luncheon coffee, and I hadn't been looking forward to it.'

Henry was feeling bewildered. He had never approved of Jane's matrimonial plans, holding the view, as so many others did, that Lionel Green was a total loss and a worm of the first water, but he had always supposed that those plans appealed to her.

'Well, this is certainly ... surprising.'

'I thought it would make you sit up.'

'You didn't tell me that this morning.'

'I didn't know myself this morning. I got the idea on the train. I had one of those moments of clear vision. It suddenly dawned upon me that there was nothing to Lionel but a profile and a couple of melting eyes. It was just his looks that had robbed me of my cool judgement. You see before you the sort of girl who gets crushes on film stars, and if I were a contortionist, I'd kick myself. I wish you weren't so good-looking, Henry, it's your only fault. Used girls in your acting days to cluster at the stage door waiting for you to come out?'

'I've no recollection of any, but perhaps I just wasn't noticing. So everything's all right, is it?'

'Everything's simply fine, except that I can't get rid of the feeling that there must be something wrong with my intelligence to have ever given me the idea that I was in love with Lionel, and I'm darned glad I found out in time that I wasn't. What I shall be looking out for from now on is someone short on male beauty but long on honest worth. I suppose infatuation with profiles and melting eyes is a sort of measles we poor dumb girls have to go through, and the great thing is to get it out of the system as soon as possible. Well, that's the Jane Martyn story, Henry, and I finished it just in time, for if you look to your left, you will see the vicar approaching. I'll leave you to entertain him.'

'I'll get rid of him as soon as I can. Oh, and I was forgetting. That book I promised to lend him.'

'*Deadly Earnest* by Thomas Hardy alias Bill Hardy alias Adela Bristow. Very interesting chap, Henry. He used to pick lemons. Where is that book of his?'

'I left it in the picture gallery.'

'I'll find it.'

Henry's interview with the vicar did not last long. All the latter wanted was to ascertain whether, like Tennyson's Sir Walter Vivian, he would all a summer's day give his broad lawns until the set of sun up to the people, people in this instance meaning the village school children and the Church Lads Brigade, and Henry's ready acquiescence completed that portion of the conversation. By the time Jane returned they were chatting amiably of the prospects of the Sussex team in the county cricket championship. The appearance of Jane broke the thread. The vicar departed with the book under his arm and Henry, turning to Jane, was surprised to note that the cheerfulness of so short a while back seemed to have left her. In its place was a gravity, as if some untoward happening during her brief absence had given her a shock of some kind.

It was not long before she enlightened him as to what was troubling her. Like Kelly, she believed in the direct approach.

'Henry,' she said, 'that man Stickney has stolen the Beau's paperweight.'

2

Expecting that this curt announcement would have a powerful effect on her audience, she was not disappointed. Henry's reaction was all that she had anticipated. On receipt of the news he would, she presumed, start violently, and this was precisely what he did. He could indeed scarcely have started more violently if a bradawl had come through the seat of the deck chair in which he was reclining and impaled his lower slopes to the depth of an inch and a quarter.

He was thinking unhappily how strange it was that three reasonably intelligent people like Wendell, Kelly and himself could plot a plot and be perfectly satisfied that it was what Algy would have called cast-iron, when all the time there was a flaw in it which should have stood out as plainly as a Palm Beach suit at the Eton and Harrow match.

He saw now that it had been madness to embark on the Operation while Jane was still in the house. They should have held everything until she left at the end of her vacation. For though not unduly inquisitive, she was always in and out of the picture gallery – with a pang he recalled that on this occasion he had actually sent her there – and no turf accountant would have given any but the shortest odds against her discovering the absence of the Beau's paperweight sooner or later.

The problem that faced him now was what to do about it. He had of course the option of telling the truth, always an agreeable thing to do if one can be sure there will be no subsequent regrets, but a moment's thought told him that this would be injudicious. Hitherto he had always found Jane pleasantly broadminded, but it was more than possible that the slight whiff of dishonesty in the Paradene-Stickney project would bring out the prude in her, causing her to take the censorious view. She might, in a word, veto the whole enterprise and when Jane vetoed a thing, it stayed vetoed, for she was a determined little creature and long ago had learned the lesson that a woman who keeps on talking can always get her way.

And even if broad-mindedness prevailed and she stamped the venture with the seal of her approval, it would be perilous to put her in possession of the facts. Girls may mean to keep things to themselves, but too often, even for the best of them, the strain becomes too much and top secrets are poured out in the strictest confidence to an intimate female friend. And one knows what intimate female friends are like. Tell them anything in the strictest confidence, and you might just as well arrange with the B.B.C. to have it broadcast on their Light Programme.

Thus Henry, this way and that dividing the swift mind. Reaching finally the decision that reticence was best, he managed to emit an adequate gasp of amazement and horror, and Jane proceeded with her narrative.

'When I was up in the picture gallery getting the book, I happened to look at the case where the heirlooms are, and the paperweight wasn't there. And it's no good asking me if I'm sure, because I am. It was gone.'

Here, of course, was where Henry should have eased the situation by saying it had been sent to the cleaner's, but this simple device did not occur to him, and Jane continued.

'And obviously the only person who could have taken it is Mr Stickney.'

'Oh, now come!' said Henry. He said it feebly. It was the best he could do, but even he realized that it was none too good. Jane brushed aside his weak bleat with a flick of the hand.

'Well, who else is there? If there's a valuable French eighteenth-century paperweight in a house and also in that house a man known to be passionately addicted to the collecting of valuable French eighteenth-century paperweights and one day it's found that the valuable eighteenth-century paperweight is missing, on whom does suspicion rest? And it's no use saying that Stickney is an honourable American gentleman who would scorn to dip into other people's paperweights. He is a collector, and everybody knows that where the things they collect are concerned collectors have no scruples. The only way to prevent them scooping up something they've taken a fancy to is to keep it nailed down. And even then you can't feel really safe.'

In the face of this remorseless reasoning it was useless for Henry to continue arguing for the defence. Perry Mason might have found something telling to advance in rebuttal, but he was more the Hamilton Burger type. He admitted that the evidence did seem to point rather noticeably in Mr Stickney's direction.

'Extraordinary,' he said, mopping a brow heated by emotion.

'What's extraordinary?'

'That a man like Stickney should have done such a thing.'

'Nothing extraordinary about it,' said his ruthless niece. 'I'll bet he's doing it all the time. Probably every paperweight he's got was swiped from some house he stayed at. That's why he's able to live on Park Avenue. His collection doesn't cost him anything. Well, what steps do you propose to take?'

Henry winced. The word had reminded him of Duff and Trotter, purveyor of fine wines and foods. He replied that he did not see how he could take any steps, and if Jane had been less pretty, one would have said that she snorted.

'You mean you're going to let this thug get away with it?'

'I don't think you ought to call him a thug.'

'What better term would you suggest? Hoodlum? Yegg? Rat of the Underworld? We ought to have got on to him right away. Hercule Poirot would have. He'd have had him tabbed the moment he wormed his way into the house. And do you know what he would have done when he found that paperweight was missing? He'd have gone to him and taxed him with the theft and told him he had three seconds to disgorge before the police were sent for. And that's what you must do.'

'I can't. Good heavens, I can't do that.'

'Then I will.'

The bradawl might have been playing a return date, so marked was Henry's reaction to these appalling words. The thought of what would be the effect on Wendell Stickney in his extremely disturbed state of mind of his host's niece suddenly introducing stolen paperweights into the conversation, paralysed him in every limb. Already, what with a guilty conscience and thinking he saw private detectives behind every bush, his fellow-conspirator was on the verge of a nervous breakdown. Such an action on Jane's part could not fail to complete the process. He pictured Mr Stickney clutching at his throat, uttering a choking cry and falling over in a more than usually severe conniption fit. His imagination continuing to take a morbid turn, he seemed to see the hastily summoned doctor putting away his stethoscope with a grave face and pronouncing that life was extinct.

'No, no, NO!' he cried. 'You mustn't say a word to him.'

'Why not?'

Inspiration descended on Henry. At long last he remembered the telling argument he should have used at the outset. His voice, which throughout this exchange of ideas had resembled that of a diffident sheep, took on a sudden firmness and rang out like a clarion.

'Because he's thinking of buying the house, that's why not. I told you when I said I was going to invite him here, that I was hoping I might be able to persuade him to take this ghastly white elephant off my hands. It's touch and go. Obviously, then, the last thing I want to do is antagonize him, and if you think it wouldn't antagonize him to be accused of going about the place stealing paperweights, you're very much mistaken. He'd pack and leave two minutes after I'd brought the subject up. So you can see how out of the question all this talk of taxing him is. I don't care what Hercule Poirot would have done, you don't catch me doing it, and if you start doing it, young Jane, I'll skin you with a blunt knife and dip you in boiling oil. We'll just have to let him keep that damned paperweight and enter it in the books as a business loss. And now I really must be going in. Letters to write, lots of important letters. Ought to have written them days ago.'

For some minutes after he had left her Jane sat motionless, chafing as only a spirited girl who likes to get her own way can chafe when baffled and thwarted. Then she rose. Recognizing the situation as one with which she was not competent to deal alone, she had decided to seek an adviser, someone who, bringing a fresh mind to the dilemma, might have something of value to suggest, and she immediately thought of Bill Hardy. Their acquaintance had not been a long one, but it had been long enough to enable her to form a very favourable opinion of his qualities. Level-headed he had seemed to her, sensible and practical.

He should, she thought, be back by now, and if back presumably at the Beetle and Wedge. She started to walk there without further delay.

3

Henry, making for the house, had almost reached it when a musical 'Hi' from the terrace announced the presence there of Kelly, and a moment later she joined him on the gravel drive.

He stared at her, amazed. It seemed to him incredible that with all the worries and anxieties and problems that were currently popping up all over the place like rocketing pheasants, anybody could look so serene and unmoved. She appeared to be under the impression that there were no such things as worries and anxieties in the world, and her opening words explained this peculiar attitude.

'I've some good news for you, Hank,' she said, and his nervous system took a sudden turn for the better. 'And when I say good news, that's understating it. It'll have you dancing around on the tips of your toes and strewing roses from your hat. Wendell's going to buy the house.'

Henry tottered. Ashby Hall seemed to flicker before his eyes like an early silent motion picture. It was as though, pursuing the policy which had proved so successful in the case of her late husband, she had conked him with a paperweight. He said in a throaty voice charged with emotion:

'Say that again!'

'You deaf or something?'

'No, but I love the sound of it so. Kelly, this is terrific. Think what this means. We'll be able to live for the rest of our lives in Majorca or the Channel Islands, or one of those places where you can get along on next to nothing.'

'That thought struck me too.'

'He was really definite about it?'

'Quite.'

'Was anything mentioned about price?'

'No, we didn't get that far, and there, Hank, is where you want to be careful and watch your step. Not having known him long, you probably look on Wendell as a dreamy artistic character with a mind above money, but he isn't like that at all. He's nobody's pushover when it comes to a business deal. He takes after his old man there. Give him the slightest chance and you're sunk.'

'I won't give him the slightest chance.'

'Well, mind you don't.'

'I can hardly wait to start the round-table bargaining. Did you have a tough time persuading him?'

'Not after I touched on the Loretta angle.'

'The what was that?'

'I brought his sister Loretta into the conversation. I told him he'd never feel safe till he was out of her sphere of influence, so what he ought to do was buy this joint and settle down on this side. He could collect paperweights just as well over here, I said, and she couldn't get at him as long as he stayed in England. She never comes to England on account of she's got a Pomeranian dog she's crazy about and she'd have to leave him behind or put him in quarantine, and nothing will make her do that. You buy Ashby Hall, Wendell, I said to him, and you've got it made. That's what turned the scale. It just shows, doesn't it, that nothing is put into the world without a purpose, not even Loretta's Pomeranian.'

'It certainly does,' said Henry.

They fell into a thoughtful silence, musing on the inscrutable ways of Providence.

Chapter Nine

1

As Algy sat in the Beetle and Wedge's lounge, looking out on the High Street and sipping whisky and soda, it would perhaps be an exaggeration to say that his brow was sicklied o'er with the pale cast of care, but he was far from being his usual debonair self. Bill's abrupt departure had disconcerted him a good deal. It had shown him that all his admirably phrased arguments had failed to move his friend from his decision to stay away from Ashby Hall. A man whom argument has convinced does not go upstairs and take baths, he remains where he is and talks things over. It was plain to him that his ingenious plan of having Bill establish himself at the Hall and pave the way for him to fraternize with the opulent Stickney was not going to materialize.

Since leaving school Algy had not devoted much time to the study of the Scriptures, and the stories of the Old Testament had to a great extent passed from his mind. Had this not been so, he would now have been thinking how close was the parallel between his own predicament and that of Moses on the summit of Mount Pisgah. Moses had looked wistfully at a promised land which he was never to reach. He in his mind's eye was gazing with equal wistfulness at a promised millionaire with whom there seemed no chance of ever talking business. It was a galling state of affairs and it is little wonder that he found the whisky and soda turning to ashes in his mouth.

He thought with a good deal of bitterness of his Uncle Henry, the prime obstacle on his road to riches. Where Algy was concerned, the attitude of the Squire of Ashby Hall was that of a bird which has been much shot over and is resolved, if possible, to avoid a repetition of the experience. Their previous relations had left Henry Paradene with the well-founded fear that Algy, if allowed to come within speaking distance of him, would somehow talk him into parting with money. He was fond of him and had no objection to sending him an occasional five pounds, but in the matter of not having him in the house he was adamant.

And only by getting into the house could Algy win to wealth. He was no pessimist, but it was beginning to look to him as if that wealth was not going to be won to. You cannot borrow money from millionaires if you never meet them.

So as he sat there, he was snorting sadly from time to time, just as one imagines Moses must have snorted, and it was as he gave vent to his feelings in this way for perhaps the fifth time that Jane came into the lounge.

Although with so much on his mind he would have preferred to be alone, the better to concentrate, he was not ill-pleased to see her. Between them, as so often happens with a brother and a sister who believe in candour in their dealings with each other, there had always existed an affection which no plain speaking could mar. He might allude to her as a squirt and a microbe, but he yielded to no one in his appreciation of her many excellent qualities, and when, as she had been known to do, she told him that he reminded her of Wimpy, the well-known moocher in the Popeye the Sailor series, there was no animus behind her words.

So now he greeted her with warmth, not actually going so far as to rise from his chair, but monitoring to her cordially to take the one adjoining it.

'Hullo, bacillus,' he said. 'Where did you spring from?'

Jane replied that she had returned a short while ago from a brief visit to London.

'I'm looking for Bill Hardy. Have you seen him?'

'We were chatting together only a moment ago. He's gone to have a bath. What do you want him for?'

'I want his advice.'

'With ref. to what?'

'Oh, something that's come up.'

'A problem?'

'Yes.'

'You'd better place it in my hands. When it comes to solving problems, Bill isn't in my class. He lacks my flair.'

Jane reflected. It might well be, she felt, that there was something in what he said. Though never blind to his numerous defects, she had always recognized his ingenuity, even if too often it merely consisted of thinking up ways of avoiding work. Even Henry was compelled to admit that he was a young man who knew all the answers. She decided that there could be no possible harm and that there might be some advantage in taking him into her confidence.

'It's like this,' she said.

Algy listened attentively as her tale unfolded. It had to be explained to him at some length how the Beau's paperweight differed in value from the ordinary run-of-the-mill paperweights which you bought for an insignificant sum at Woolworth's, but after he had grasped this he was intelligent and understanding.

'So you think Stickney has pinched the thing?' he said as she concluded her narrative.

'Who else could have? He collects paperweights.'

'I'd hate to have that engraved on my tombstone. "Here lies Algernon Martyn in the hope of a glorious resurrection. He collected paperweights." Visitors to the cemetery would think I must have been potty. However, there it is. So we pencil Stickney in as the Bad Guy. But though he's the Napoleon of Crime, Henry can't denounce him because he's hoping he'll buy the Hall. Correct?'

'Quite correct.'

'Well, it's obvious what must be done.'

'Not to me.'

'My good squirt, it leaps to the eye. Pinch the thing back.'

'Pinch it back?'

'That's right.'

'Without his knowing?'

'Exactly.'

'How?' said Jane, and Algy conceded that she had a point there.

'It would have to be carefully done, of course, and to ensure

118

success you would have to have someone of my gifts to do it. But how can I take on the job while Henry has this absurd fixation about not letting me into the house? But perhaps if you explained to him that my presence there would result to his advantage, he would relax his rigid views. If I came and offered to lend a hand, he'd probably be touched.'

'That's what he's afraid of.'

Before Algy could comment on this remark, a rattling sound as of clashing tin cans made itself heard in the street outside the window at which they were sitting. It was the taxi that met all the trains, and it was plain that though at its maximum speed it would have difficulty in arriving in time to meet the one which was its objective, for it was already at the platform and obviously about to resume its journey.

'Oh, there's Kelly,' said Jane. 'She's missed it.'

'Kelly?'

'Mr Stickney's aunt. She was going to London to get him a valet. I told her she ought to allow plenty of time because you can't rely on the station taxi. It's one of those temperamental ... I wish you wouldn't do that,' she said, speaking peevishly, for Algy had brought his fist down on the table with a sudden bang very afflicting to the nerves. 'What's the matter?'

'Did you say valet?'

'Yes, he's just fired his.'

'And she was off to London to get him another?'

'Yes.'

'How well do you know this Kelly? I mean, if you advised her to do something, would she do it?'

'She might.'

'Then go and catch her at the station and after commiserating with her for missing her train tell her it's really all for the best because you can save her the fatigue of a journey to London because if it's a valet she's after there's no need for her to bother, because by a most extraordinary coincidence you've just run into your late Uncle Cedric's valet –'

'My late Uncle *who*?'

'Cedric. Used to be Bishop of Oswaldtwistle. You can't go wrong making him a Bishop. And his valet has happened to

119

come down here for the shrimping or whatever they do in these parts, and you looked in at the Beetle and Wedge for a gin and tonic, and there he was. And owing to the Bish having gone to reside with the morning stars he's out of a job at the moment and will be only too glad to fill in till Stickney can get a regular –'

'Algy!'

'You spoke?'

'What on earth are you talking about?'

'You mean you aren't abreast?' Algy was amazed. 'I thought the penny would have dropped instanter. I'm telling you to tell this Kelly to give me the vacant job of Stickney's valet.'

'What!'

'Valet. Stickney's. Vacant job of. Then Henry can't keep me out of the house, and I shall be in a position to collect that paperweight at my leisure.'

'But –'

Jane paused. Her initial impression that the strain of modern life had become too much for her brother was beginning to pass, leaving in its place a growing conviction that the scheme he had formulated was an extremely shrewd one. No doubt Mr Stickney was concealing his ill-gotten loot somewhere in his room, and a valet's opportunities for searching an employer's room are limitless.

Only a small doubt marred her enthusiasm.

'But could you get away with it?'

'Of course I can get away with it. I was always playing butlers and valets in the Footlights shows at Cambridge.'

'Were you good?'

'Colossal. Don't worry about my ability to give a smooth west end performance.'

'And it'll only be for a day or two.'

'Less. You remember how good I was at hunt-the-slipper when we were kids. I don't expect it'll take more than about ten minutes to find the missing object. Why the silvery laugh?'

'I was thinking of Henry's face when he sees you.'

'Ah yes. A bit contorted it will be at first, no doubt, but there's good stuff in Henry and he'll soon pull round. But we mustn't sit here chatting about Henry's face, much as I admire it. Off with you to contact Murphy.'

'Kelly.'

'Murphy or Kelly, this is no time for splitting straws. Tell her to go to the Hall and brief Stickney and send the taxi back for us. She'll understand that you and your Uncle Cedric's valet will want to talk over old times for awhile before rejoining the human herd.'

When Jane returned, it was to announce that all was well.

'Kelly was delighted. She says Come on right up.'

'Excellent. Then all I have to know ... Oh, a small point. How the hell does a woman get a name like Kelly?'

'It was her mother's maiden name. She was a Miss Kelly.'

'Oh? How simple it all seems when you explain it. Well, as I was saying, all I have to know is what sort of bloke is this Stickney. I mean, is he one of those ruthless tycoons who crush men like flies, or is he a mild non-crusher? The point is a vital one. In the former case I shall be obsequious, in the latter supercilious and superior, sneering at him and dominating him. I don't want to get the wrong conception of the part.'

'Well, I haven't seen much of him, but he looks pretty mild to me. The thing I know about him that will interest you is what Kelly told me, that he won't stand a valet fussing over him. He had an agreement with Clarkson, the one who's just left, that Clarkson was to get double wages for leaving him absolutely alone. He won't have a valet telling him what to wear and so on.'

'Then why does he have a valet?'

'Kelly explained that. He has a strongminded sister who makes him have one.'

Algy drew a deep breath.

'I'm glad you told me that. I was intending to tell him that I expected to be in full charge of his wardrobe, dictating to him in the matter of suitings, shirtings, sockings and pyjamaings. Thanks, pipsqueak, for your invaluable help. I now see my way, and I am prepared to give you attractive odds that in a relatively short time the man will be as wax in my hands, if not eating out of them. The thing'll be a love feast.'

2

For a few minutes after the taxi had returned and they were on their way Algy sat in meditative silence, running plans and strategy over in his mind. He had ample time to do this, for after that impetuous dash to the station the driver and proprietor of the vehicle was going through what might be called a cooling off process. Two bursts of velocity in a single afternoon were more than he was prepared to demand of his Arab steed. In response to Kelly's repeated inquiries as to whether his darned jeep couldn't do more than three miles an hour he had given of his best, but it had been with a heavy heart. He knew too well that anything in the nature of motor rally stuff was apt to shake vital organs loose.

Algy's thoughts ran on the pleasantest lines. To the problem of the re-stealing of the paperweight he gave little of his attention. It was a trifling task to which he could attend any time when he had an idle moment. Once a hunt-the-slipper expert, always a hunt-the-slipper expert. What really mattered was that he would now be in constant association with a millionaire to whom money meant nothing, and if he could not extract a paltry sum like five hundred pounds from such a one when he had a sound commercial proposition to place before him, he was not the man he thought he was.

If he had had any misgivings, Jane's story would have dispelled them. It had revealed this Stickney as quite definitely a crook, and it probably required someone with a touch of the crook in him to look favourably on a venture which might be considered by a purist to border on sharp practice. It was not that his own conscience was not clear. In holding up these Croxley Road building boffins he knew that he was morally justified. They had no business coming defiling a charming oasis like Valley Fields with their beastly blocks of flats, and it would do them a world of good to get a sharp lesson. Nevertheless, he could not disguise it from himself that in the enterprise he was contemplating the straightlaced might possibly detect a certain fishiness, and he was glad that he would be dealing with one whose views were so liberal as were those of

Mr Stickney. A man who goes about purloining other people's paperweights can scarcely afford to set himself up as a censor.

It was in uplifted mood that he turned to Jane, ready now to pass the time in agreeable conversation. Remembering that she had told him that she had just returned from a visit to the metropolis, he made her trip the subject of his opening words.

'What took you to London in weather like this?' he said, and when Jane replied that she had telephoned Lionel Green and asked him to give her lunch, his disgust and disapproval were manifest.

'You ought to have your head examined,' he said, not for the first time. It had been his constant advice to her for years. 'What a way to pass a summer afternoon! What you see in that blot on the London scene beats me. What has he got to offer a girl?'

'Great charm, don't you think?'

'No, I don't.'

'And he's terrifically handsome.'

'Bah!'

'Lovely voice, too.'

'You're making me sick.'

'In fact, you might say he has everything. Except at the extreme lower end. Have you ever noticed his feet?'

'A busy man like me hasn't time to go peering at L. P. Green's feet. Something wrong with them?'

'Something seriously wrong. They're of clay. I only discovered this quite recently, and when I did I decided not to marry him.'

For the second time that afternoon a fit of choking deprived Algy of speech, showing him once more the imprudence of allowing strong emotion to coincide with his inhaling. Before, it had been mirth that had caused this; now it was a sudden gasp of astonishment. The crisis past, he stared at her, amazed.

'You're not going to marry him?'

'No.'

'It's really off?'

'Right off. Banns definitely forbidden. That wedding cake will not ring out. So no need for any more brotherly anxiety.'

It was not often that Algy kissed his sister, for one does not want girls getting intoxicated with rapture and starting to give themselves airs, but he did now with a good deal of heartiness. He felt she had earned it.

'This is certainly tidings of great joy.'

'I'm glad you're pleased.'

'But what gave you this belated gleam of sense?'

'It's not important.'

'No, it doesn't matter why you came out of the ether and saw L. P. Green for what he is. The great thing is that you did. It was bound to happen some time, and it's lucky it didn't happen in the vestry after the ceremony. Well, this will be wonderful news for Bill.'

'Bill?'

'He'll go singing about the Beetle and Wedge like the Cherubim and Seraphim.'

'Why?'

'Why, do you ask? Because he loves you, child – loves you with a passion that threatens to unseat his very reason, and now you're at liberty to accept his addresses. He –'

'Algy!'

'Hullo?'

'Is your reason unseated?'

'Never firmer in the saddle.'

'Then why are you talking drivel like this?'

'I cannot recall talking any drivel.'

'This nonsense about Bill being in love with me.'

'Nonsense? You think that's what it is, do you? Then let me tell you that I had it straight from the horse's mouth. Viz, his.'

Jane's eyes, as always when some new line of thought was opened before her, had become large and round.

'But he's only met me a couple of times.'

'Once was ample. He took one look at you, 'twas all he had to do, and then his heart stood still. I believe it frequently happens that way. Amazing you didn't spoil it. I thought girls were always supposed to get on to it in a flash when a man was in love with them. Yes, Bill fell for you with a dull thud

124

the first time he saw you, and you can imagine what a nasty jolt it gave him when he found you were engaged to L. P. Green. You should have seen him when he came back this afternoon. He looked like a corpse that had been in the water several days. He couldn't speak, he couldn't crack a smile, all he could do was go upstairs and take a bath. And I shouldn't be surprised if when in the tub he didn't weigh the idea of shoving his head beneath the surface and ending it all. Well, that's the Bill situation. Think him over carefully, always bearing in mind that the match has my hearty approval. For never forget that whoever you marry will be my brother-in-law, and in the matters of brothers-in-law I am choosy, even finnicky. Bill will be exactly right. Grab him. It's an opportunity that may not occur again. Ah,' said Algy, as the taxi rattled to a halt at the front door, 'here we are at the old shack, where Stickney awaits me. Bring him on and let me at him. I feel alert, confident. Something tells me that this is going to be my finest hour.'

3

There now occurred a slight hitch in the programme. Jane, dispatched to find Kelly in order that she might introduce his new valet to Mr Stickney, returned with the information that the latter had gone to the village to buy chocolate bars – an extravagance which, as Jane observed with some bitterness, considering that he was stealing paperweights all the time instead of paying for them, he could well afford.

Algy said he liked the sound of this. It seemed, he explained, to humanize Mr Stickney, showing him in a rather lovable light.

'It bears out what you were saying about his mildness. If he eats chocolate bars, he can't be the type of employer who chews broken glass and tenpenny nails and is ferocious with those on his payroll. Milk chocolate?'

'That's the sort I bought for him.'

'So I shall find him full of the milk chocolate of human kindness. Well, what do we do now?'

'Wait, I suppose. At least, you do. I'm going down to the lake to have a swim.'

'I wish I could be with you, but I suppose it would hardly be the correct thing in the circumstances. One must not step out of character. Where do you suppose Henry is as of even date? I am looking forward to seeing him again.'

'He's probably having a bathe, too, on an afternoon like this.'

'Getting all clean and fresh for his guests, eh? The right spirit,' said Algy approvingly. 'Then I shall go for a stroll on the lawn. No doubt we shall meet there.'

'I'd love to see that meeting.'

'It shall be fully described to you in God's good time.'

Jane's conjecture was accurate. Henry was leaving the lake just as she reached it. After the exchange of a few words he started to return to the house with a song on his lips, one of the songs he had sung nightly and at matinées in the musical comedy phase of his career, for what with the thought of his love for Kelly and the recollection of what she had told him about Mr Stickney's plans for the home of his ancestors he was in festive mood. No lark could have carolled more blithely, and he would undoubtedly have continued to carol indefinitely, had not his eye been caught by a spectacle that pulled him up with a jerk just as he was half-way through the chorus. It was the spectacle of a tall thin young man smoking a cigarette on the lawn, a young man who bore the most extraordinary resemblance to his nephew Algy.

A second and keener glance having shown him that the resemblance was due to the fact that the other actually was his nephew Algy, he bounded forward full of justifiable wrath, his air that of an uncle who intends to demand an explanation.

'Algy! What the devil are you doing here?'

Algy turned with a welcoming smile. He was always glad to see the head of the family and regretted that his opportunities of having that pleasure were so limited.

'Ah, Henry, I was wondering when you would be entering left centre or whatever you used to call it in your sock and buskin days. You look very fit and rosy.'

'Never mind how I look!'

'But I do mind how you look,' said Algy, gently rebuking. 'You're health is always a matter of the greatest concern to me. I was just saying to myself before you came up "I wonder how Henry is. Well, I trust. No dizzy spells, no night sweats, retchings or nauseas." Capital to see you so plainly in the pink. It relieves my anxieties.'

'How often have I told you I won't have you here?'

'I'm sorry, I've lost count. But I'm afraid you're going to have to have me – as long as Mr Stickney is your guest.'

'What!'

'As soon as he returns from buying chocolate bars, he will be engaging me as his valet.'

'What!'

'You always told me I ought to get a job, and this is it. But the thing goes deeper than mere valeting. Have you seen Jane?'

'I saw her for a minute.'

'Didn't she explain?'

'What?'

'Our plans for your benefit. She came to me at the inn and told me all about the paperweight.'

'What?'

'You do keep saying "What!" don't you. In the kindliest spirit I think you ought to try to correct the habit. Yes, about Stickney pinching it. I've come to pinch it back for you, a task which as his personal attendant I shall find absurdly simple. He's bound to have tucked it away somewhere in his room, and I shall always be in and out. I expect to be able to restore it to you in record time. I wouldn't do it for everyone, mind you, because there's always the chance of finding him breathing down the back of my neck as I search through his belongings, which you will agree would be not a little embarrassing, but despite this odd habit of yours of shunning my society and not allowing me in the house I have always wished you well and am prepared to take the risk.'

'Oh, my God!' said Henry. He was thinking.

The last thing he would have wished to do, had circumstances been other than they were, was to reveal his business secrets to anyone like Algy, in whose discretion he had little or no confidence, but as so often happens circumstances were not other than they were. In the matter of the paperweight the situation had reached a deadlock. Wendell Stickney stoutly refused to take it to the post office himself, nor would he allow his host to take it. But surely he would have no objection to his valet acting as carrier. It would probably strike him as the ideal solution.

The moment was one for quick decision, and Henry recognized it as such. He hesitated no longer.

'Algy!' he cried.

Algy raised a deprecating hand.

'I know what you're going to say, Henry. You are about to tell me that you wish there were more nephews like me in the world, because that's what the world stands in need of.'

'No, I'm not.'

'You're not?' said Algy, hurt. 'Of course, I want no thanks, but I did think a little gratitude would be in order.'

'Can you keep a secret?'

'I can't remember ever having done so, but I could try.'

'Then listen,' said Henry, and prefacing his words with the injunction that Jane must never hear of this, for if she did she would infallibly bully him into abandoning the enterprise, he proceeded to place the facts before him.

It was with a new respect for his uncle that Algy listened. He was telling himself that he would never have credited him with the vision and know-how required for such a transaction – still less with the cool intrepidity that enabled him to contemplate without a tremor a deal where one false step meant a spell in the calaboose. His enthusiasm grew with every word, and when the narrative drew to a conclusion, he said that it would be a genuine pleasure to him to lend a hand in such a worthy cause.

'Let's just review the bidding. Coldness of the feet prohibits Stickney from posting the parcel himself.'

'Yes.'

'And he won't let you do it.'

'No.'

'So you want me to entrust it to the mails.'

'Exactly.'

'Consider it entrusted. I may have my limitations, but I'm quite capable of carrying a parcel to a post office. But a thought strikes me,' said Algy. 'Now that the pinching sequence is off, what's the point of my taking on this valet job? I was never really keen on the idea and was doing it purely to oblige you. True, Jane tells me that the duties of a man serving under Stickney's banner are light, but what I ask myself is are they light *enough*? Under the best of conditions being a valet always means work. There are shoes to be shined, trousers to be pressed. No, what you do is introduce me as your nephew who's come to spend a few weeks with you at your country residence.'

His use of the expression 'a few weeks' caused a quick chill to run through Henry, but there was, as Algy had told Jane, good stuff in him and his dismay was only momentary. With any luck, he reflected, he should be able to get rid of his nephew long before the expiration of that period of time. He had done it before, and he could do it again. It only required perseverance and the will to win.

'Very well,' he said, 'but listen, Algy. Once that paperweight is in Stickney's bank I shall have his cheque for a thousand pounds –'

'And very nice, too.'

'– and any attempt on your part to share the wealth –'

'My dear Henry!'

'– will be met with a firm refusal. I'd like that thoroughly understood. You don't get a smell of it.'

Algy reassured him with a wave of his cigarette holder.

'Of course, of course, of course. Have no anxiety whatsoever, Henry. I wouldn't dream of trying to bite your ear. All I want is your hospitality for a week or so.'

'Why?'

'I hope to interest Stickney in a business proposition.'

'Oh? Well, in that case –'

'Exactly.'

A thought struck Henry.

'But how about the valet?'

'Eh?'

'Stickney's expecting one. How do we explain –'

'The fact that he's not here? Perfectly simple. We tell him that he came, took one look at the house and was off like a nymph surprised while sunbathing. Quite plausible, surely. Suddenly catching sight of Ashby Hall would understandably cause a sensitive valet to feel that he was better elsewhere.'

Henry turned his head and having regarded his ancestral home in silence for a moment said that he supposed that that would meet the case.

'Then I'll only have to explain to Kelly.'

'And I to Jane. I'll tell her I lost my nerve and backed out. I doubt if she'll be surprised. But who is this I see approaching?'

'Where?'

'Coming up the drive.'

'Oh, that's Stickney.'

'Well, well. So that's the Stickney of whom I have heard so much. Give him a hail, and when you've introduced me pop off and leave us,' said Algy, and when Henry had followed these instructions and left him alone with Wendell he proceeded to make himself as charming to the latter as only an impecunious young man can to a certified millionaire. He had found his first sight of Mr Stickney most encouraging. Here, he could see at a glance, was no ruthless tycoon. If this man had ever crushed anyone like a fly, there was certainly nothing in his appearance to indicate it. He had on the contrary the air, than which nothing is more agreeable to a hopeful borrower, of being the sort of man who is easily talked into parting with five hundred pounds as a temporary loan.

Mr Stickney, on his side, was also extremely cordial. The afternoon, as has been stated, was warm, and though the walk from Ashby Hall to the village was not a long one, it had been long enough to engender a powerful thirst. This he had corrected with a series of beers at the Beetle and Wedge, and the beer brewed by the Beetle and Wedge's landlord was of an exceptional strength, having much of the authority of the audit ale in vogue at Oxford colleges, two glasses of which are calculated to lower the strongest-headed reveller below the table. The result had been to dissipate the fears and anxieties which

130

had been preying on his mind so much of late. He was feeling gay and carefree and wondering why he had ever allowed himself to be intimidated by a private detective who was probably incapable of detecting a bass drum in a telephone booth. Even when Algy, having covered the topic of the weather, mentioned that his Uncle Henry had drawn him into the closed circle of his and Mr Stickney's little secret society, he remained nonchalant.

'Oh, you know about that?' he said affably.

'And heartily approve,' Algy assured him. 'I think this business of not being allowed to sell heirlooms is perfectly ridiculous. I've often said so.'

'Who to?' asked Mr Stickney, holding a match to the fountain-pen he had taken from his breast pocket in the erroneous supposition that it was a cigar, for he had decided to resume his smoking. Men who indulge too freely in the Beetle and Wedge's homebrewed beer are always making mistakes like that.

'Oh, various friends of mine.'

'You have friends, have you?'

'Lots of them.'

'So have I, mostly in the Collectors Club. That's a club in New York, called the Collectors Club because its members are collectors. You have to be a collector to become a member, and by collector I imply a man who collects things.'

'Quite.'

'I don't know what you mean by quite, but that is how the matter stands. If you're a collector, you join the Collectors Club, which enables you to meet other collectors.'

'And a very good arrangement, too,' said Algy cordially.

'So I have always thought. But my sister Loretta says it's an unnecessary extravagance and is always at me to resign. You ever met my sister Loretta?'

Algy regretted that he had not had that pleasure.

'Odd,' said Mr Stickney. 'She goes everywhere. Stout woman.'

'Yes?'

'Very stout. Can't keep her off the starchy foods. This darned cigar won't draw.'

'I think it's a fountain-pen.'

'Ah, that accounts for it. I was wondering. What was I telling you about?'

'You were saying you had a stout sister.'

Mr Stickney ruminated for a moment.

'I withdraw the word stout, substituting in its place the adjective obese. She married a man named Pound in the insurance business. You probably know him?'

'I'm afraid not.'

'You don't seem to know anyone,' said Mr Stickney, showing signs of being about to enter the belligerent phase.

'But I'm extraordinarily good at posting paperweights,' said Algy, feeling that it was time the conversation was jerked back to fundamentals, 'and I'm posting yours first thing tomorrow morning.'

'No, you're not,' said Mr Stickney, 'and I'll tell you why. Do you know a place called Aldwych? It's somewhere in London.'

'Yes, I know Aldwych.'

'I bank there.'

'Oh, yes.'

'And I've decided to take the paperweight to London myself and deposit it with my bank. Then there'll be no risk of it getting lost in the mail.'

'But how about the private eye?'

'What about him?'

'I thought you couldn't make a move because you were so scared of him.'

Mr Stickney barked scornfully.

'That rat? I regard him with quiet contempt. He'd best keep away from me if he knows what's good for him. Yes, that's what I'm going to do, and now I must be leaving you and going and lying down. For some reason I'm feeling kind of sleepy. Probably the warm weather.'

As Algy watched him make for the house, weaving a little in his walk, he was conscious of a growing uneasiness. This very unexpected decision, he realized, had left his position in his Uncle Henry's home more than a trifle shaky. It was as a poster of parcels that Henry had reluctantly consented to his presence there, and now it seemed that there were no parcels to be posted. This being so, how long would it be before he was ejected from Ashby Hall like the Peri in Mr Moore's poem who had the same experience in Paradise?

It was unquestionably a problem of the kind which Sherlock Holmes would have described as being not without certain points of interest. His first encounter with Wendell Stickney had gone so like a breeze that it seemed to him that he needed only a few more of the same sort to enable him to grapple the man to his soul with hoops of steel, and it would be bitter if he got the bum's rush before this could be accomplished. With knit brow he paced the lawn, and it was as he paced that Henry emerged from the house, dressed now in the conventional costume of the English country gentleman.

Henry seemed cheerful, like a man who has had a weight lifted from his mind.

'I've just seen Stickney,' he said. 'Ran into him in the hall.'

'Oh, yes?'

'He's decided to take that paperweight up to London tomorrow.'

'So he told me.'

'Which means that there's nothing to keep you here now, so you will be leaving shortly.'

'You're pushing me out?'

'That's right. Sorry, but you know my views.'

Algy's face suddenly lightened. Inspiration had come to him. Inspirations affect different people in different ways. The mathematician Archimedes, when he had one, leaped from his bath shouting 'Eureka!' Algy merely lit another cigarette.

'Aren't you forgetting that I know your guilty secret?' he said. 'How about if I blazoned it forth to the world?'

Henry reeled. He stared incredulously.

'You wouldn't!'

'Of course I wouldn't – if sober. I wouldn't dream of it. But suppose some night I got a bit pie-eyed and babbled indiscreetly? Don't you see how much safer you would feel if I were here where you could keep an eye on me and watch that

I didn't exceed. Only so could you feel really easy in your mind. How about it? Do I stay on?'

The cheerful glow had faded from Henry's face.

'Very well,' he said in a low voice. Once again, as had so often happened before, he was forced to the realization that he was in the presence of a nephew who knew all the answers.

4

It was getting on for the dinner hour when Bill reappeared in Beetle and Wedge circles. His bath had not occupied more time than baths usually do, but after drying and clothing himself he had lain on his bed for some two hours busy with his thoughts.

These, dealing as they did almost exclusively with L. P. Green, had little or no therapeutic effect on his gloom. The more he mused on L. P. Green, the more remote seemed the prospect of any girl betrothed to him deciding to do the sensible thing and detach herself from him. True, only a handful of the six hundred and forty-three pupils at the ancient foundation at which he had been educated had excelled L. P. Green as stinkers, but girls are sadly apt not to allow themselves to be influenced by a man's moral shortcomings. The outer crust rather than the soul within is what appeals to them, and it was futile to pretend that outer crust of L. P. Green was not exceptional. And all he, Bill Hardy, had to pit himself against it was an honest heart and a certain rude skill at getting cats down from trees.

With a sigh he forced himself at length to rise, to brush his hair and to descend the stairs. The prospect of having to talk to Algy all through dinner in the lounge afterwards was not an inviting one, fond though he was of him. He craved for solitude, and that to his surprise was what he got. Neither in the bar nor in the lounge was Algy among those present. He had either been snatched up to heaven in a fiery chariot or he had met his Uncle Henry and been invited by him to dine at Ashby Hall. Neither solution seemed probable, but it was difficult to think of any other. Having waited for a quarter of an hour, he gave him up and went in to his solitary meal. And it was as he took his seat that he noticed that lying beside the napkin which the Beetle and Wedge provided for each of its clients, folded by loving hands into the shape of a water lily, was a letter.

On leaving Valley Fields, Bill, who had expected to be some considerable time in Ashby Paradene, had arranged with the local post office to have his mail forwarded, for there was always a chance that included in it would be a communication from the New York literary agent to whom he had sent his novel of suspense. And, he perceived with a thrill, here it was. With trembling fingers he tore open the envelope and proceeded to master its contents.

They did not disappoint him. Literary agents' letters are always masterpieces of polished prose, but this one stood by itself on a pinnacle of perfection. He could not remember when he had read anything to touch it for human interest and purity of style.

The waitress came to his table and offered him the choice between boiled beef and chicken pie, with a kindly word of warning that the shrewd diner would do well to avoid the latter, and Bill said, 'Yes, boiled beef, please,' though what he would have liked to do was tell her the whole wonderful story.

'Mabel,' he would have liked to say, 'do you know what? I sent this book of mine to this chap Brinsley Mereweather in New York, never dreaming that anything would come of it, and you'll be astounded to hear that not only has he landed it with a prominent firm of publishers but has actually sold it as what he calls a one-shotter to a magazine for the stupendous sum of four thousand dollars. I don't suppose anything so sensational has ever occurred before in the whole history of English literature, and if you need a new hat or a mink stole or anything like that, buy it and chalk it up to me.'

It was only after he had disposed of the boiled beef and the unpleasant-looking blancmange which followed it that he descended like a shooting star from the pink cloud on which he was riding and remembered that his life was a blank. Brinsley Mereweather might do his utmost and so might the prominent firm of publishers, but strive though they might to brace him up they could not alter the fact that in next to no time Jane Martyn would be going around under the alias of Mrs L. P. Green.

Sombrely he refused cheese and went into the lounge to brood.

So intent had he been on the opening portions of the letter that he saw now, as he re-read it, that he had omitted to note at the bottom of the page the word 'Over', and turning it now he found that Brinsley Mereweather had added a postscript.

In it he strongly recommended Bill to lose no time in coming to New York, so that he could study the American market and meet editors and publishers and generally consolidate this promising opening success. Only so, said Brinsley, could the good thing be pushed along as it should be pushed.

It seemed to Bill the most admirable suggestion. His years in America had given him a great fondness for the country, and if ever there was a time for returning there, this was surely it. The conventional thing for hopeless lovers in England had always been to go to the Rocky Mountains and shoot grizzly bears, but meeting editors and publishers would be an excellent substitute.

It would mean getting an overdraft from his bank in Aldwych but on the strength of this letter that could no doubt easily be arranged.

He decided to attend to it on the morrow.

Chapter Ten

1

When a man is about to take a train journey of forty-five miles and proposing to return the same afternoon, it is unusual for his friends and relations to accompany him to the station and see him off, this pretty gesture of concern being more generally reserved for longer and more poignant partings. But such was Wendell Stickney's agitation on the following morning as he faced the ordeal of coming out into the open with the Beau's paperweight on his person that both Henry and Kelly felt it imperative to be at his side to give him moral support. It was their view that, left to himself, he would weaken and bolt off the course.

His *obiter dicta* on the platform showed them how wise their decision had been. His conversation dealt almost exclusively with the menace of the private detective whose dark shadow had been weighing on him so long. Who could say, he reasoned, that the fellow was not even now lurking somewhere in the vicinity all ready to swoop, having divined by some devilish flash of intuition that he and the paperweight were on their way to London together?

Useless for Kelly to assure him that if there had been a detective on the platform, she would have noticed him, and for Henry to deny that the man existed. Nothing they could say had the slightest therapeutic effect on his morale. Only the thought of depositing his treasure at his bank nerved him to the fearful task with which he was confronted. His whole attitude was that of a particularly nervous spy who has had assigned to him the carrying of top secret papers through the enemy lines.

Considering how airily Wendell had spoken to Algy of this detective as 'the rat' and with what fortitude he had stressed the quiet contempt with which he regarded him, his present frame of mind may at first sight seem inconsistent, but there was a ready explanation for his change of heart. When talking to Algy he had been filled almost to the brim with the Beetle and Wedge's homebrewed beer, under the influence of which some of the mildest characters in Ashby Paradene had been known to assert that they could lick anyone in the house, and the passage of time had caused its stimulating effects to evaporate, leaving him once more the timid fawn of pre-beer days.

This being so, conversation could not but be strained, and it was with relief that Henry heard himself hailed by a hearty voice and, turning, saw his friend Wade-Pigott approaching their little group.

Claude Wade-Pigott of the firm of Bates, Wade-Pigott and Pollard was a plump man of medium height, florid features and an unfailing geniality which expressed itself mainly in a stream of the latest stories he had heard on the Stock Exchange. He always reminded Henry of the low comedians of his musical comedy days who had called him 'laddie' and begged him to stop them if he had heard this one, well knowing as they spoke that nobody within the memory of man had ever stopped them telling a story.

'Going to London, Harry?' said Claude Wade-Pigott.

'No, just seeing my friend Stickney off. Mr Stickney, Mr Wade-Pigott.'

'How do you do?'

'Mrs Stickney. Mr Wade-Pigott.'

'How do you do?'

'You off to work, Claude?'

'No, I'm playing hooky today. Taking my sister's kids to the Zoo. We're meeting at the Savoy. You going in that direction, Mr Stickney?'

'I am going to my bank in Aldwych,' said Mr Stickney with an involuntary glance about him lest this dangerous admission might have been overheard by ears trained to catch the slightest whisper.

'Fine. Capital. Splendid,' said Claude. 'So we shall be together all the way.'

The train rolled in, farewells were exchanged, and the travellers took their seats, Mr Stickney clutching his parcel in a feverish grip, his companion running over in his mind the one about the Bishop and the lady snake charmer.

Ever since the dinner party at which Henry had been a guest, Claude Wade-Pigott had been longing for someone he could tell stories to, and in Wendell he had found the captive audience he required. For say what you will to the detriment of those who run the English railway system, their practice of dividing trains into small compartments renders conditions ideal from the viewpoint of the raconteur. Only by opening the door and jumping out could Wendell have avoided listening to the Niagara of anecdotes which Claude poured out on him. Before they had covered a dozen miles he had heard so many that it seemed to him, as he tried to muster up a wintry smile each time the narrator reached the punch line and slapped him on the leg, that the only one missing was the one his Aunt Kelly had told him about Mrs Heavenly Rest Johnson's brother-in-law Ephraim.

But though primarily a specialist in the type of story known as Stock Exchange, Claude could strike a more serious note. He had often worried quite a good deal about his friend Henry's finances, and he welcomed this opportunity of discussing them with another of Henry's circle, on whom he could rely to be sympathetic.

'You know Paradene well?' he said, changing the subject after placing Wendell in possession of the facts in the matter of the Bishop and the lady snake charmer.

Wendell, always exact in his speech, replied that the word 'well' perhaps overstated it somewhat, but he had seen enough of Henry while at Ashby Hall to have taken a great liking to him.

'A charming personality,' he said.

'One of the best,' said Claude.

'My aunt is very fond of him,' said Wendell.

'Anybody's aunt would be,' said Claude.

It was at this point that Bill came in from the corridor, seated himself in the opposite corner and relit his pipe.

2

One uses the prefix 're' because he had lit it a few moments earlier and a little further along the train, to be informed instantly by a man who looked like an undertaker that this was not a smoking compartment. He had withdrawn immediately to go in search of a compartment that was, and the first he came to was the one occupied by Wendell and Claude Wade-Pigott.

He was still breathing a little heavily as he sat down, for owing to oversleeping himself it was only by a last minute dash that he had caught the train. The door indeed had actually closed on Claude and Wendell before he hurled himself into it.

Claude gave him the brief unfriendly glance which the travelling Briton gives the intruder on his privacy and then ceased to recognize that he was there, but the glance of Wendell resembled more that which a bird bestows on a snake whose eye it has caught. He stared at him, frozen in his seat, and ceased to do so only when compelled to by Claude Wade-Pigott's resumption of his monologue.

'They don't come any better than Henry,' he was saying, and Wendell, speaking with difficulty, agreed that No, they didn't. His mind was in a turmoil, his heart thumping almost audibly. Seldom had he been nearer to one of those conniption fits to which, according to his Aunt Kelly, he was so addicted. Through a flickering mist he seemed to see two Claude Wade-Pigotts, and one would have been more than ample.

'I'm sorry for Henry,' said Claude.

'Oh?' said Wendell.

'Yes, Stickney, sorry for him.'

'Oh?' said Wendell.

'You've probably gathered from the look of that place of his,' said Claude, gathering speed, 'that he's pretty hard up. It started with one of his ancestors in the eighteen hundreds who spent money like a drunken sailor – remind me to tell you the one about the vicar's wife and the drunken sailor – and there were other ancestors later on who played the market and didn't have much luck, so what with one thing and another about all Henry got when he succeeded to the property was that ghastly house and a lot of heirlooms. I keep telling him he ought to sell some of them.'

Wendell swallowed uncomfortably.

'I thought it was against the law.'

'It can be done.'

'But they send you to prison.'

'Not if you work it properly. I know a fellow who did it. Naturally I won't mention names, but this fellow – call him Smith – had an old house in Shropshire which was bursting with heirlooms. Historic place. People used to come from all over the world to look at it, particularly Americans, and one of them, a millionaire, stayed with him one weekend, and when he left Smith had a bright idea. He sold those heirlooms for a nice bit of money to a dealer he could rely on to keep it under his hat, and when the trustees found them gone, he said Yes, he'd noticed they weren't there and had wondered why. He had come to the conclusion, he said, that they must have been pinched by an American millionaire who had been staying with him. Knowing of course that the American bloke was safely back in the States, where they couldn't get at him. I don't suppose the trustees believed him for a moment, but there was nothing they could do, and Smith lived happily ever after. He explained the sudden change for the better in his finances by saying he had had a wonderful run of luck on the turf lately. Good thinking on his part, don't you agree?'

Wendell did not reply. His eye had swivelled round again to the opposite corner, and he observed with interest that the detective, producing a notebook, had begun to write rapidly in it. An author, even if his life has become a blank, is always an author, and Bill was anxious to record this very promising plot for a short story on his tablets before it faded from his mind. He was sure it could be worked up into something which Brinsley Mereweather would be able to sell without difficulty to one of his cronies in America's editorial chairs.

'But I was speaking of the vicar's wife and the drunken sailor,' said Claude Wade-Pigott, bringing the conversation back to more important matters.

3

Back on the home front, while these stirring happenings were taking place on the front line, an atmosphere of quiet relief prevailed. Both Henry and Kelly, though limp and exhausted from the efforts to still Wendell Stickney's apprehensions and inject into him a modicum of the spirit that wins to success, were experiencing the relaxed peace that comes to prominent officials who have achieved without disaster the launching of a battleship. Or perhaps it would be better to say that their emotions resembled those of anxious parents who, having foiled all their young son's attempts to make a break for liberty, have managed to get him safely on the stage to recite Curfew Shall Not Ring Tonight at the village concert. There had been moments on the platform of Ashby Paradene station, when it would not have surprised them to see Wendell take to himself the wings of a dove and vanish into the Beetle and Wedge for more of that hostelry's life-saving beer. Nothing could go wrong now, they felt. They had got him on to the train. It was the surmounting of that first hurdle that was all important.

Only Algy struck the jarring note. Not wishing to wound Kelly by casting aspersions on a relative by marriage, it was to Henry that he struck it. His acquaintance with Wendell Stickney, he said, was only in its opening stages, but he had seen enough of him to form the opinion that it was absurd to suppose that a man of his mentality could possibly essay the task of conveying a French eighteenth-century paperweight from Ashby Hall to a London bank without disaster. And when Henry, who resented having cold water thrown on his hopes and dreams, told him he was talking drivel, he recommended him to wait. Just wait, he said, just you wait, and supported his view by telling Henry about Wendell and the fountain-pen. A man, he reasoned, who cannot tell the difference between a fountain-pen and a cigar is not a man in whom complete confidence can be placed.

Henry had not long to wait. The afternoon was still young when a car drew up at the door of Ashby Hall and from it emerged a Wendell Stickney in even worse shape than the Wendell Stickney of a few short hours ago. His eyes were glassy, his breathing stertorous, his general demeanour that of one who has recently been caught in some kind of machinery. Even such a man, the chauffeur of the car was probably thinking, so faint, so spiritless, so dull, so dead of look, so woebegone, drew Priam's curtain in the dead of night and would have told him half his Troy was burned.

'Algy,' said Henry some little while later, approaching the hammock in which his nephew lay and rousing him with a finger in the lower ribs from the refreshing sleep into which he had fallen, 'you were right.'

Algy sat up, rubbed his eyes and prepared to listen.

'Right, did you say? How do you mean right? You mean about Stickney?'

'Yes. He's back. He didn't make it.'

Algy's mouth opened, but he closed it considerately before an 'I told you so' could escape. He could see that Henry was deeply stirred, and he had no wish to rub salt in his wounds.

'Messed everything up?'

'Completely.'

'Tell me the whole story in your own words, omitting no detail, however slight,' said Algy.

Henry brooded darkly for a moment.

'Well, you saw him when we started out this morning. He was jittery then.'

'Quivering like an aspen, if I remember rightly.'

'At the station he got much worse. Kept bleating about this detective who was following his every move. I began to doubt whether we would be able to get him on the train. However, a friend of mine turned up and they went off together. And mark this, Algy. They had a compartment to themselves. Nobody else was there. We saw that distinctly. Yet Stickney solemnly asserts that the journey had scarcely started when he looked up and saw the detective in the opposite corner.'

Algy pursed his lips.

'I don't like that.'

'Nor did Stickney.'

'I believe medical men have a name for that sort of thing. It would be interesting to go into Stickney's case history.'

'A delusion, of course.'

'Undoubtedly. Sometimes they hear voices.'

'You don't hear anybody's voice when you're with Wade-Pigott.'

'The friend of whom you were speaking?'

'Yes. On the Stock Exchange. Lives in that house across the valley.'

'Did he, too, observe the phantom?'

'I don't know.'

'It would probably have been invisible to all except Stickney. So what then?'

'Wade-Pigott started telling a story about a man he knew who had heirlooms and sold them and when the trustees came to make inquiries he claimed they had been stolen by an American who had been staying with him.'

'An unfortunate subject to hit upon. How did the disembodied spirit take it?'

'This was where Stickney nearly expired. He says he whipped out a notebook and jotted it all down, to be used, he assumed, as evidence later. He told me he froze from the soles of the feet upwards.'

'One can see how he would, he having a conscience as sore as a sunburned neck. What is it Shakespeare says about a guilty conscience? It doth something, Shakespeare says, but just what eludes me at the moment.'

'So eventually they arrived at Victoria.'

'The phantasm still one of the gang?'

'So Stickney says. He says it sat there to the end of the journey, smoking a pipe and looking out of the window. At Victoria they appear to have lost touch. Stickney was headed for his bank, which is in Aldwych, and Wade-Pigott for the Savoy, and they took the Underground, to avoid the traffic, and there didn't seem to be any signs of the spectre, Stickneys says, though of course he kept a sharp eye out for it. At the Savoy he had a drink with Wade-Pigott, and then started walking to his bank. It was there, he says, that the spectre rejoined him.'

'At the bank?'

'At the bank. He asked to see the manager and was told he would have to wait. So he waited, and suddenly out of the manager's private office came the Spectre.'

'Probably been arranging for an overdraft.'

'That finished Stickney. He was out of there like a flash, taking the paperweight with him, and didn't stop running until he found a motor place, where he hired a car and came home. He is now lying in a darkened bedroom with cold compresses on his forehead. So what do you make of it? I ought to tell you that this is not the first time this sort of thing has happened. Only last night he swore that he had seen this detective of his lurking on the lawn. Kelly went out to investigate, and of course there was no one there. I think the man's potty.'

Algy nodded.

'He sounds pretty potty to me. On the evidence which you have submitted I would say that he would walk into any loony-bin in the land, and they would reserve the royal padded cell for him. Well, this shows how foolish it was to deviate from the original plan of having me take the thing to the post office and entrust it to the mails. If you'll abstract it from Stickney, I'll go and do it now. The heat is oppressive and I had been hoping to continue catching up with my sleep, but when it's a matter of playing the game and not letting the side down, Algernon Martyn has no thought of self.'

Chapter Eleven

1

A young man who, having decided to leave England and sail for America, has come up to London to make the preliminary arrangements for his trip and has found everybody he encounters most kind and helpful, might be expected to be in a mood of happiness and tranquility, and it is with regret that the historian has to record that Bill Hardy, as he sat in the train that was taking him back to Ashby Paradene, fell very short of achieving this state of Nirvana. Spiritually he was far below par, and falling lower every moment.

His bank manager had agreed to give him his overdraft without so much as raising an eyebrow. Nobody could have been more obliging than the representative of the White Star-Cunard. And that fellow on the morning train had given him the nucleus of a darned good story. He had, in short, everything that should have resulted in what the French call *bien être*, but it was all rendered null and void by the thought of L. P. Green and his approaching nuptials. As the train puffed its way through the outlying suburbs, it had suddenly occurred to him that Jane might invite him to the wedding and he would have to give L. P. Green a pair of candlesticks or a fish slice.

He was still reeling as he contemplated this gruesome possibility, as far as it was possible for him to reel while seated, when his attention was drawn to the fellow-passenger in the corner opposite him.

He was a man of middle age, rather good-looking in a seedy way, and until this moment he had been reading an evening paper and giving every indication of intending to keep himself to himself as a decent British traveller should. But now Bill was horrified to see that the fellow was shooting covert glances at him and showing unmistakable signs of being about to start a conversation. And even as this fear gripped him the other proved that his apprehensions had been well founded by leaning forward and clearing his throat.

'Mr Hardy, isn't it?' he said.

Bill was appalled. A stranger breaking in on his reverie would have been bad enough, involving, as such an outrage must, tedious talk of the weather and the political situation, but here apparently was, if not a friend, at least somebody he had met and would be expected to remember. And he had no recollection of ever having seen the man.

'Binstead,' said his companion, tapping his chest.

Bill's embarrassment reached a new high. The name, evidently relied on to refresh his memory, had conveyed absolutely nothing to him. He had been at school with a boy named Binstead, but that Binstead would be at least twenty-five years younger than this Binstead, besides having bright red hair, an adornment lacking in the Binstead before him. This Binstead – call him Binstead Two – was brown on top, turning to grey. He shifted uneasily in his seat, and some beads of perspiration bedewed his brow.

'Odd, running into each other like this,' said Binstead Two. 'How's Mr Martyn?'

Bill started. This time the name had brought illumination. Memory returned.

'Good Lord!' he cried. 'You're the broker's man!'

'That's right,' said Binstead Two. 'Though Bailiff is the term more generally employed. Broker's men today are found only in pantomime. Yes, I had the pleasure of meeting you at your residence in Valley Fields. I work for Duff and Trotter.'

Bill's relief was so profound that all thought of trying to suppress this conversation at the outset had left him. Now that he no longer had to grope for clues as to the man's identity, he was prepared to continue it till the train stopped at Ashby Paradene.

'Nice job?' he said.

Binstead – Bill remembered now that he had heard Algy address him as Clarence – pursed his lips, apparently thinking that the adjective 'nice' was not the one Gustave Flaubert, that exact stylist, would have chosen.

'Well, it's a living. You know what's wrong with it? Cooks.'

'Cooks?'

'The risk of getting emotionally entangled with them. It's always difficult to find anything to say to cooks, once you've exhausted the subject of food, and when there's an awkward pause, you're very apt to ask them to marry you. If you knew how often I'd got engaged to cooks and only saved myself by flight, you'd shudder. I live in daily dread of meeting one of them again. Wake up at night screaming sometimes. Still, as I say, it's a living.'

'How did you get into it?'

'Oh, influence, influence. I used to be on the stage. Musical comedy. Bit parts and understudies. But most of the time I was resting. Found it almost impossible to get a shop. Drink,' said Clarence Binstead regretfully. 'Couldn't keep off it. Which reminds me. You haven't by any chance a flask on you?'

'I'm afraid not.'

'Too few people have these days. It was different in my acting career. One never went thirsty on those tours. That was when I was understudying Harry.'

'Harry?'

'Harry Paradene. He was the second juvenile.'

'That's curious.'

'Why?'

'I'm living at a place called Ashby Paradene.'

'That's where I'm headed for. Harry came into some property there. Place called Ashby Hall. I'm bringing him the fatal papers. Representing Duff and Trotter. And there you have another thing I don't like about this job of mine. It isn't pleasant to have to slip the kiss of death to a friend like Harry. Still, I suppose we'll enjoy talking of the old days,' said Clarence Binstead philosophically, 'and considering that his Duff and Trotter bill runs to something over a hundred and fifty quid for wines, spirits and liqueurs, there ought to be plenty to drink.'

He licked his lips in anticipation of the coming treat. Bill sat silent. He was thinking of Jane. Engaged to L. P. Green and forced to associate all the time with broker's men, what a life for her. And even if you called them bailiffs he could not see that that made it any better.

He awoke from his reverie to find that the train had stopped at Ashby Paradene.

'You don't happen to know the way to Harry's place, do you?' said Clarence Binstead as they left the station.

'Straight up the road till you come to some big iron gates. You can't miss it.'

'How far?'

'About a mile.'

'In this weather! And me with a sore toe. Oh, well,' said Clarence Binstead, and set out on the arduous journey.

Bill went to the Beetle and Wedge, and took a chair in the lounge. His spirits were now at their lowest ebb. Brinsley Mereweather had done his best to raise them and had for a time succeeded, but now melancholy had taken over again. Under certain conditions the selling of a one-shotter to a magazine can be only a momentary palliative.

He had been in the lounge some little time, staring at nothing, when the door flew open and Algy came in.

2

Bill regarded him morosely. It was plain from a mere look at him that he had achieved the *bien être* denied by Fate to better and more deserving men and was sitting on top of the world with a rainbow round his shoulder. He bubbled over with cheerfulness, and when one is a toad beneath the harrow, which was Bill's unpleasant position, one resents effervescence in others.

'So there you are,' he said.

Mabel the waitress appeared for an instant at the service door, and Algy blew her a debonair kiss.

'Yes, here I am, Bill, and glad to see your bonny face again.'

'What on earth became of you?'

'Oh, I'm dug in at the Hall, and my affairs are prospering greatly. I have been able to do Stickney a signal service, and he and I are on kissing terms already. He couldn't love me more if I were the finest paperweight.'

Bill was amazed.

'But I thought your uncle wouldn't have you in the house.'

'So did he. I had to be very persuasive. But he finally saw the light.'

'I'll tell you something else he's going to see very soon.'

'Clarence Binstead, you mean?'

'You know about that?'

'I met him as I was coming here, and he informed me of his mission. I must say my heart bleeds a bit for Henry. If only he had taken me into the home earlier, I could have warned him that Duff and Trotter were not men to be trifled with. Still, an occasional sock in the eye like this is no doubt good for him. But how do you know about Clarence?'

'We travelled down together.'

'Have you been to London?'

'Yes.'

'You're practically commuting these days. What took you there?'

'I went to buy my passage on the boat.'

'How do you mean, the boat? What boat?'

'The one that leaves for New York next Wednesday. I'm going to America.'

Algy gasped.

'You're *what*? Did I hear you say going to America?'

'Nothing to keep me here, is there?'

'There most certainly is. You mustn't dream of doing anything so cloth-headed as going to America. But good Lord, you don't know, of course. You haven't been apprized.'

'What about?'

'The squirt. The germ. Her engagement. It's off.'

It seemed to Bill that the lounge of the Beetle and Wedge, though solidly built, had broken into one of those modern dances. There was an advertisement of somebody's whisky on the opposite wall, and he distinctly saw the lightly clad girl who featured in it perform a series of uninhibited wiggles. Even Mabel, who had reappeared, was flickering.

'What?'

'Yes, no wedding bells for L. P. Green. She's given him the heave-ho, and not before it was needed. She's now open once more to consider offers.'

Bill drew a deep breath. The lounge ceased to gyrate.

'When did this happen?'

'This afternoon, apparently. She went up to London to see him, and came back freed of all encumbrances. I don't wonder you're much moved, but there's just one thing you've got to bear in mind before you start waving your hat and dancing the dance of the seven veils, and that is that you won't get anywhere unless you establish contact with the girl. You must see her constantly. You must be always at her side. You must model your tactics on those of a porous plaster. I am doing all I can to get the bacillus thinking along the right lines. I have told her you love her –'

'What!'

'Everybody says "What!" around these parts. I had to speak to Henry about it only this afternoon. Yes, I told her you loved her with a passion that threatened to upset your very reason and, as I say, that will have helped, but it isn't enough. Your personal touch is required. We must put our heads together and think of some way of introducing you into the home, so that you can do your wooing at short range instead of by remote control. It won't be easy, mind you. Henry is already shaken to his foundations by having me about the place, and the chances of him taking you on as an added guest are virtually nil. He's funny where my friends are concerned. Neurotic, you might say. He shudders at the thought of giving them so much as bed and breakfast. On several occasions I've tried to sell him the idea that having me and a few of my pals down for the weekend would brighten his lonely life, but no business resulted. You would be far more likely to obtain access if you put on false whiskers and said you had come to inspect the drains. In fact, I thought of that as a possibility, but then I decided –'

He broke off. A travel-stained figure was entering the lounge, the travel-stained figure of Clarence Binstead.

3

That was the first thing anyone would have noticed about Clarence Binstead, that the warmth of the day and the unaccustomed exercise in which he had been indulging had caused him bodily discomfort. He was moist and dusty, and it was plain that his sore toe was paining him. But to a closer observer it would have been manifest that he was also not at his best spiritually. His air was that of a man whose soul as the result of a shock of some kind is not at rest. Kelly, that expert diagnostician, would have recognized all the symptoms of an impending conniption fit.

His advent occasioned considerable surprise in both Bill and Algy. One does not expect a broker's man or bailiff, when on the trail, to come homing back to his base with mission unaccomplished any more than one would be prepared for similar behaviour on the part of a bloodhound after it has got its nose down to the scent. It is an axiom that bailiffs, like the Canadian Mounted Police, always get their man, and this cannot be done by tottering into the lounges of country inns and begging those already there in a hoarse voice for God's sake to give them a drink.

Bill, always considerate, hastened to attend to this request while Algy was still asking questions, and presently Clarence, having like the stag at eve drunk his fill, became coherent enough to utter the word 'Coo!'.

'I needed that,' he said, wiping a trembling lip. 'Do you know what?'

His hearers replied that they did not, but were all eagerness to learn what.

'We supposed by this time,' said Algy, 'you would be snugly installed at Ashby Hall, the life and soul of the party. Didn't you get there?'

Clarence shuddered and informed him briefly that he had got there all right.

'Coo!' he said again.

'Don't tell me Henry kicked you out? I thought the whole idea was that you weren't allowed by law to kick broker's men out.'

'I never saw him.'

'He must have been there.'

'I dare say he was, but I didn't wait to find out.'

Algy clicked his tongue impatiently. This broker's man seemed to him to be talking in riddles, and it annoyed him. Nobody likes having to listen to broker's men talking in riddles.

'I find you obscure, Clarence Binstead,' he said rebukingly. 'Come to the point and let your Yea be Yea and your Nay Nay. You got to the Hall? Yea or Nay?'

'Yea.'

'Good. We make progress. You then went in?'

'No, I didn't.'

Algy pounced like a prosecuting attorney on a hostile witness. 'Why not?'

'Because I heard her singing Rock of Ages.'

Algy looked at Bill as the prosecuting attorney might have looked at the jury, as though to draw his attention to the extreme fishiness of this witness's testimony.

'Who?'

'Eh?'

'Who was singing Rock of Ages?'

'The cook.'

'How do you know it was the cook?'

'Because I saw her. Listen,' said Clarence Binstead, 'I'll tell you the whole story. When I got to the house, I thought perhaps I'd better not go in at the front door, because I wasn't just an ordinary visitor –'

'Very tactful.'

'So I went round to the back. And I'd just got to the back door when I heard this Rock of Ages.'

'Cleft for me, and all that. Let me something something thee.'

'That's right. Well, I stopped and listened. "That voice sounds

153

familiar," I said to myself. "I've heard that voice before," I said to myself. There was a window alongside the door, and I peeped through, and everything went black.'

'Why?'

'Because it was her.'

'Who?'

'The cook. Scooping food out of a tin for a couple of cats.'

'You have some objection to cooks scooping food out of tins for cats?'

'They can scoop till their eyes bubble, as far as I'm concerned. But this was Mrs Simmons.'

'Yes, I believe that is the name of my uncle's cook. You know her?'

'I got engaged to her when I was serving the papers at a house I was at last June. I was telling this gentleman here on the train that I was only saved by flight.'

'Well, all this seems very odd to me,' said Algy. 'I happened to go to the kitchen this afternoon for a drink of water, and I made the acquaintance of this Mrs Simmons. She struck me as a worthy soul, if not much of a conversationalist, but I find it difficult to envisage her lighting the spark of passion in the male bosom, though one presumes that she did in that of the late Mr Simmons. What made you propose to her?'

'He always does, he tells me,' Bill explained, 'when he can't think of anything to say. It keeps the conversation going.'

Algy nodded.

'I see, I see. I also see that this has put you in something of a spot. If you go to the house and hand Henry the papers, you can't avoid encountering La Simmons with, I should imagine, disastrous results; but if you don't, you presumably lose your job, for I don't suppose you could make Duff and Trotter see the thing from your angle. You're properly up against it.'

'That's what I was thinking. I don't know what to do.'

'I can tell you. You must hand on the torch.'

'Eh?'

'To Mr Hardy here. By the greatest good fortune his one desire is to find some way of inserting himself into Ashby Hall, and this is his big opportunity. He will taken on your assignment.'

'Hey!'

It was Bill who spoke. An electric shock seemed to have
passed through him, lifting him some inches from his seat.

'You were saying, Bill?' said Algy courteously.

'You're crazy.'

'You find something wrong with the idea?'

'How could I be a broker's man?'

'It only requires pluck and perseverance.'

'I don't look like a broker's man.'

'They come in all varieties.'

'I shouldn't know what to say.'

'There's practically nothing you need say. Actions speak
louder than words, and handing Henry the papers more or less
lets you out. Think of the advantages of being installed in
Ashby Hall. Once on the spot, there are no limits to what you
can accomplish.'

'But –'

Bill paused. Stunned for an instant by this latest manifestation of Algy's clear thinking, he had begun to recover. It was
not perhaps the method he would have chosen for achieving
propinquity to the girl he loved, but he was not in a position to
be captious.

'Do you know,' he said. 'I believe you've solved the problem.'

'There is always a solution to every problem,' said Algy. 'If,
of course, you have an Algernon Martyn to find it.'

Chapter Twelve

1

Ashby Hall slept in the sunshine; Algy, more prudently, in the shade. He was taking his afternoon siesta in the hammock which was suspended beneath the big cedar on the lawn. Eventually, waking refreshed, he would go down to the lake for a swim, always a pleasant way of passing the time during a heat wave.

His thoughts before he dropped off and began to snore gently with a sound like the sawing of wood in a distant lumber-camp, had been of a nature well calculated to encourage peaceful slumber. Everything, it seemed to him, was working out precisely as he could have wished. Mr Stickney, informed of the successful entrusting to the mails of the Beau's paperweight, had shown just the proper spirit, not actually saying 'My preserver!' but leaving no room for doubt concerning his gratitude and esteem, and had gone off to London to a sale at Sotheby's a changed man, as full of beans and buck as the character in Coleridge's Kubla Khan who on honeydew had fed and drunk the milk of Paradise.

And Henry. Before long Henry was scheduled to get a shock which would jar him to his shoe soles and make his two eyes, like stars, start from their spheres, but against this must be set the fact that the experience would be of the greatest spiritual value to him, making him a graver, deeper man resolved to be more careful in the future how he ran up accounts for wines, spirits and liqueurs with tough babies like Duff and Trotter. If Henry learned the stern lesson that if you cannot pay for wines, spirits and liqueurs, you must jolly well do without them, he would have taken a long step towards becoming the well-adjusted man.

But it was as he mused on Bill that Algy felt happiest. Now

that the sinister shadow of L. P. Green had passed he could see nothing but roses and rapture ahead of him. If he and Bill, working as a team, could not play on the squirt Jane as on a stringed instrument, breaking down any sales resistance she might show and getting her thinking along the right lines, he would be more than surprised, he would be astounded. It needed only a few well-chosen words to convince the young microbe that Bill was what the doctor ordered, and well-chosen words were his speciality.

Thinking thus, Algy drifted off into slumberland.

His should have been a calm and dreamless sleep, but oddly it was disturbed by something in the nature of a nightmare. He seemed to be sitting with Mr Stickney in the lounge of the Beetle and Wedge and he had just asked him for a loan of five hundred pounds, confident of ready acquiscence on his part, when suddenly Mr Stickney, so far from writing a cheque, had lifted the golf club he happened to have with him – a number seven iron it looked like – and struck him forcibly in the lower ribs with it, accompanying the gesture with the rather mystical words 'Death to Clarence Binstead!' The shock woke him and opening his eyes he perceived his Uncle Henry at his side. It was presumably his finger rather than a number seven iron that had prodded him in the ribs. He recalled that Henry had employed this crude method of rousing him from slumber on a previous occasion.

Henry was in critical mood.

'Good Lord!' he said. 'Don't you ever do anything but sleep?'

Algy with considerable dignity rebutted the slur. He had merely, he protested, dropped off for a moment owing to the warmth of the afternoon. Henry, he said, was to be blamed for keeping the grounds of Ashby Hall so overheated.

'And anyway,' he continued, 'if one does sleep occasionally, you always see to it that one does not sleep long. I don't want to knock your hospitality, Henry, it's princely and I'm enjoying my stay immensely, but I do wish you would shake off this habit of yours of driving your index finger into your guests' ribs whenever you find them relaxing. It gets you talked about.

But perhaps I am wrong in supposing that you do it merely as an outlet for your animal spirits. It may be that there is something about which you wish to confer with me. Yes, I believe I can see speech fermenting behind that inscrutable mask of yours. You may speak freely. What's biting you?'

'Where's Stickney?'

'Ah, that I can tell you. You've come to the right place for all the latest about Stickney. He went up to London after lunch. He had two objects in mind – first to put that paperweight in a safe deposit box; second, to attend a sale at Sotheby's, where he will no doubt purchase further paperweights. Extraordinary, don't you think, his passion for the beastly things. If somebody offered you or me a paperweight, we would of course do the polite thing by giggling a bit and thanking him and saying it was just what we wanted and how did he guess, but we would be careful to lose it on our way home. Stickney, on the other hand –'

Henry did not foam at the mouth, but it was plainly a near thing. His manner, when he was able to get a word in, was febrile.

'Stop *talking*!'

'Certainly, if you wish it.'

'Stickney owes me a thousand pounds.'

'You'll get it when he returns, which will be, I imagine, when the fields are white with daisies.'

'I want it now. I was a fool. I ought to have got it from him last night.'

'Why the hurry?'

'Because when he gets back, he'll find a broker's man in the house.'

Algy was suitably astounded.

'A broker's man? A bailiff?'

'Yes. About that money I owe Duff and Trotter.'

Algy was looking grave.

'This isn't too good, Henry.'

'It couldn't be worse. Stickney has promised to buy the house –'

'You don't say! Well, heartiest congratulations.'

'– but no terms have been agreed on, and if he finds I've got a broker's man in the place, he'll knock ten thousand pounds off the asking price.'

'But why does he want the house?'

'It's the home of his ancestors. He's a sort of distant cousin. A Stickney once married a Paradene. He sent me a family tree he'd worked out. That's why I asked him here.'

'Then you have a bargaining point.'

'I would have, if this infernal broker's man hadn't turned up. He may still buy the Hall, but what good is that to me if I'm practically letting him have it for nothing. Kelly says he's a devil at driving a bargain, and this will give him his chance. Algy, what shall I *do*?'

Early in this conversation Algy had climbed out of the hammock. It had seemed to him the courteous thing. He now paced up and down, pondering.

'What sort of a fellow is this broker's man? Presentable?'

'How do you mean, presentable?'

'Could he get by as a guest?'

Henry started.

'I never thought of that! Yes, he's an ugly-looking kind of chap, but he doesn't drop his aitches.'

'Then everything is simple. You introduce him as a friend of mine.'

'By Jove!'

'I expect you're beginning to feel more and more how lucky it was that you prevailed on me to come here.'

'But would he agree?'

'Why not?'

'He'll probably expect me to slip him a tenner.'

'Well, slip him a tenner.'

'But I haven't got a tenner.'

'That's all right. I'll have a talk with him and if necessary promise him a douceur at some future date. Don't you worry. I can handle him all right.'

Henry went so far as to pat his nephew affectionately on the back, a great improvement on prodding him in the ribs.

'Algy, I take back everything I may have said in the past about you being a pest and a curse and a waster.'

'And a pain in the neck?'

'Yes, and a pain in the neck. I still think you ought to get a job and buckle down to earning your living, but nobody can say you aren't a very pleasant help in time of trouble. There's just one thing,' said Henry, as they walked to the house. 'I shall have to let Kelly in on this. She was with me when the broker's man presented his credentials. Will you come along?'

'No, I think I'll have a swim in the lake.'

'Yes, do,' said Henry. 'Just the thing in this weather.'

He found Kelly in the drawing room putting records on the gramophone, and took her immediately into his confidence.

'Kelly!'

'Yes, honey?'

'That broker's man.'

'I've been worrying myself sick about him.'

'Well, you needn't. It's all right.'

'You've murdered him and hidden his body in the west wing?'

'Something just as good. Here's the scenario. Wendell's gone to London to a sale at Sotheby's.'

'I thought I hadn't seen him around.'

'And when he gets back, I'm going to pass the broker chap off to him as friend of Algy's. It was Algy's idea. He says he can talk him into it, and I'll bet he can. He once talked me into putting three hundred pounds into a play of his. Don't you like the set-up?' he asked anxiously, for he was unable to detect in Kelly's face a glimmer of the joyful light he had anticipated. She was looking stolid and unenthusiastic. In his youth he had seen whole audiences look like that at Wednesday matinées, and the sight chilled him.

Kelly noted his concern and would have eased it if it had been possible, but the situation was too serious to permit of subterfuge.

'No, honey, I don't,' she said frankly. 'From where I sit it looks like a wash-out. We're having duck for dinner.'

Henry found her cryptic.

'Duck?'

'With peas. Suppose this guy takes his knife to them. How would that square with him being a friend of Algy's? Wouldn't Wendell raise his eyebrows and start wondering? If you're going to pass him off as anything, I'd make him vice-president in charge of cleaning the knives and boots.'

'He'd never do it.'

'Then can't you keep him under cover till tomorrow, when you'll get Wendell's cheque for the paperweight and be able to pay him off? Where is he now?'

'In the kitchen.'

'Well, tell him to stay there till the All Clear's blown. I'll go and see him now and tell him how the script reads.'

She left the room, and after a brief interval returned.

'He's not there. The butler says he went out the back door. He must be in the grounds somewhere. I'll hunt around. Oh, honey, it's too bad you had to run up this enormous bill with those Duff and Trotter guys. I ought to have stopped you, but of course I hadn't met my angel sweetie pie then.'

Her angel sweetie pie rose to a point of order.

'Dash it, I wouldn't call a hundred and fifty pounds that. Substantial, but not enormous.'

Kelly was staring.

'Did you say a hundred and fifty pounds?'

'About that.'

'Well, why the heck didn't you tell me so before. Here I've been getting all worked up and tearing my hair into ribbons, and all the time I could have given you the dough and set your little mind at rest.'

Henry, too, was staring.

'You don't mean you've got a hundred and fifty pounds?'

'More than that. In traveller's cheques, which I guess are as good as the real stuff. I'll go get them now and find this gink and hand them over and get a receipt and tell him to get the hell out of here before we set the cats on him.'

She moved towards the door. He stopped her with a hoarse cry.

'Kelly!'

'Yes, honey?'

'Don't go yet.'

'I'm in a hurry.'

'But wait just a bit.'

'Why?'

'I want to hug you till your ribs squeak.'

'Oh, in that case,' said Kelly, 'be my guest.'

2

It was with a good deal of annoyance that Algy, coming out of the house in bathing trunks and a bathrobe, all set for a cooling plunge in the lake, saw Bill immobile on the lawn as if he were posing to a sculptor for his statue. Just standing there, he said to himself bitterly. He felt like a General who, having devised a plan of campaign calling for the whole line to advance, goes into the camp and sees his troops loafing about there with cigarettes and mouth-organs, the last thing in their minds a forward movement.

'What on earth do you think you're doing, Bill?' he cried. 'A fat lot of good me getting you installed in Ashby Hall if you're simply going to bask in the sunshine like this. I thought by this time you would have been well ahead with your wooing. Those wedding bells aren't going to ring if you don't take the lead out of your pants and get a move on. And don't tell me you don't know where Jane is. She must be somewhere, and it's your job to find her.'

'Listen,' said Bill, and for the first time Algy noticed that he had the forlorn air of a man who has swallowed an oyster and found too late that it was not as juvenile as he had thought. 'It's all off.'

'What's all off?'

'Everything. I've got to leave.'

'Leave?'

'Yes, I've been paid off, and she told me explicitly to get out and stay out and not let them see my ugly face again.'

Algy was feeling that the intellectual pressure of the conversation had become too much for him.

'She? Who?'

'I don't know who she was – a tall handsome woman.'

Algy made a swift deduction. It was not a difficult one to make, for the description certainly did not fit Mrs Simmons.

'Kelly!' he exclaimed. 'It must have been Stickney's Aunt Kelly. But why would she be paying Henry's bills? Gadzooks!'

'What?'

'Just an exclamation of surprise. Pay no attention. Do you think she's in love with Henry?'

'I couldn't tell you.'

'That must be it. They're going to get married.'

'I hope they'll be very happy, but that doesn't alter the fact that I've got to clear out without seeing Jane.'

The gravity of the situation was not lost on Algy.

'This calls for constructive thought, Bill. Don't speak for a moment. I want to bend the brain to this. I think I'll walk up and down a bit.'

'Do.'

'There's only one thing to be done,' said Algy, having walked up and down a bit. 'I shall go to Henry and tell him all – i.e. that you're a thoroughly good egg in spite of being in broker's man clothing and came here merely with the object of pressing your suit, and I shall plead with him to do the decent thing and let you stay on. It may work, or it may not work, but it's worth trying. Go down to the lake and wait for me there. It's through those trees.'

3

It took Algy from five to seven minutes to outline the position of affairs to Henry and solicit his views on the situation, and during those minutes Bill remained standing where he was, deep in thought. Then, roused from his meditations by the sound of the station taxi as it clattered up the drive, he came to life and started to walk to the lake, as directed.

Henry, his views solicited, gave them crisply. They were not of a nature calculated to uplift his nephew. In a few terse words he refused to offer his hospitality to any friend of Algy's. It was, he said, a matter of principle, and he was particularly inclined to abide by his rules in the present instance because the mere thought of his niece Jane marrying into Algy's disreputable circle of friends filled him with horror and revulsion. This Bill of whom he spoke might, as he insisted, be superior to the general run of the dregs of humanity with whom Algy consorted, but that, he was sure his nephew would agree, was not saying much. No, said Henry with the firmness of the Russian representative at the United Nations issuing his hundred and eleventh veto, a thousand times no, and Algy, having said that he considered Henry subversive, pig-headed and lacking in the most elementary humanity, withdrew.

He had passed through the front door and was descending the steps, when the station taxi drew up and Wendell Stickney emerged.

Enough has been written of Wendell Stickney in this chronicle to show that he was a mercurial man, given to changing moods. Now up, now down, as you might say. Under the influence of the Beetle and Wedge's homebrewed beer, for instance, he had been practically radiant, his only fault a slight tendency to incoherence. Yet the following morning, according to Henry, had found him a victim to a severe attack of combined jitters and heeby-jeebies. You never knew what to expect. Sometimes placid and cheerful, at other times giving a realistic impersonation of a sufferer from St Vitus dance. It lent to his personality a jumpiness which, while interesting, was calculated to disturb his intimates.

He appeared now to be completely at his ease. It was with unshaking hand that he paid the proprietor of the station taxi his just dues, and there was not a tremor in the finger he pointed at Bill, who, having been walking slowly and pensively, was still in sight.

'See that fellow?' he said. 'When did he get here?'

'This afternoon.'

'Know who he is? That's the detective guy I was telling you about.'

His nonchalance astounded Algy. It was as though he were pointing out some object of mild interest by the wayside, some cow or perhaps a rabbit which had engaged his attention.

'You seem very calm about it,' was all he could find to say.

'And I'll tell you why I'm calm,' said Wendell. 'I see my way now to dealing with the fellow, drawing his fangs and rendering him powerless for evil. Thanks to Otis J. Peabody. I guess you don't know Otis? He's in oil. Been in oil ever since I've known him.'

Algy said the pleasure of meeting the human sardine had been denied him.

'We both belong to the Collectors Club in New York. I have an idea I told you about the Collectors Club?'

'Yes, I remember. You collect things.'

'That's right. Otis collects old English warming pans. I ran into him at Sotheby's this afternoon, and why I should have told him all about me and that paperweight I can't think, unless I got the notion somehow that he might have something to suggest. But thank goodness I did, because he clarified the whole situation. You know what he said when I mentioned that there was a private eye nosing around and giving me nervous breakdowns?'

Algy said he did not.

'He told me not to give it a thought. He assured me that all these private eyes have their price. Square him, he said. That's what he said. Square him.'

'Not a bad idea.'

'A darned good idea. It solves everything. I was thinking that maybe you would act as my agent.'

'I shall be delighted. It would save you an unpleasant interview.'

'Most unpleasant. Where was he off to?'

'Going to have a look at the lake, I think.'

'Go after him.'

'I will. How much shall I offer him?'

'I was thinking of a hundred dollars.'

Algy's frown showed plainly that he was far from being in agreement with this modest proposal. Lending emphasis to the frown, he shook his head disapprovingly, and Wendell was quick to understand.

'Not enough, you think?'

'Not nearly enough.'

'Then what would you suggest?'

'Five hundred pounds,' said Algy, who had had another of his inspirations and felt that there is a tide in the affairs of man which, taken at the flood, leads on to fortune.

Wendell winced as if bitten in the leg. His jaw fell a little. He was a wealthy man, but it is always the wealthy who have that parsimonious streak in them.

'That's a lot of money.'

'Worth it to be sure of getting rid of him. I must tell you about this fellow. He was staying at the inn while I was there and we got talking one night, and he told me all about himself. It seems that ... you don't know Valley Fields, do you?'

'Never heard of it.'

'It's one of the London suburbs, and they are starting to build there a good deal, and apparently some concern wants to put up a big block of flats in a road called Croxley Road.'

'So what?'

'I'll tell you what. Plumb spang in the middle of where these people plan to build their flats is a house belonging to a man whose name I've forgotten, and the point is that they can't make a move till they've bought him out. All clear so far?'

'Clear as mud.'

'Well naturally if he was able to go on holding his house, he could stick the price up.'

'Of course.'

'But he can't. He's rolling down to Rio or somewhere almost immediately, and that's where your private eye comes into the picture. The Rio-roller has given him an option to buy the house, if he can pay five hundred pounds by the end of this week, the rest to be coughed up later. I think the man's asking eight thousand, and it will be child's play for your private eye to bump the price up to twenty thousand, provided – always provided – he can raise the initial five hundred. So you can see how favourably he would look on your offer of that sum.'

Nothing could have exceeded Wendell's enthusiasm.

'He'd grab it and be out of here right away. You wouldn't see him for dust.'

'Exactly. So though, as you say, five hundred pounds is a lot of money, it will be money well spent.'

'You bet it will. I'll write a cheque this very moment. Come along with me to Paradene's study.'

'Better make it out to me.'

'You think that would be best?'

'And I'll endorse it over to him.'

'Sure. That's the simplest way. And you'll go see him?'

'Immediately.'

'Maybe you could get him to shade his price some?'

'He needs the full five hundred.'

'But he probably has some savings.'

'I doubt it.'

'No harm in putting it up to him.'

'No, I'll do that, but I very much doubt if he'll see the suggestion in a favourable light. You know what these private eyes are,' said Algy. 'They drive a hard bargain.'

4

Bill, meanwhile, passing through the belt of trees, had reached the lake.

It was a lake of considerable size. One of the many things Beau Paradene, when building the Hall in the eighteen-twenties, had resolved not to economize on had been the sheet of ornamental water which the custom of those days held indispensable to the country seat of a man of property. Its construction had called for the services of a small army of diggers and paving the floor with stone had not been cheap, but he had a soul above all sordid consideration of expense. The result was in every way satisfactory to him, especially after he had caused a few statues to be scattered around and had added the marble temple without which no gentleman's ornamental water was thought complete.

To Bill it seemed like something out of a fairy story book, needing in his opinion only one thing to make it perfect, the presence of the girl he loved. And this omission was speedily rectified, for as he stood gazing at the temple across the water a voice spoke behind him, affecting him in much the same manner as the cough of Clarkson on a memorable occasion had affected Wendell Stickney and his fellow conspirators.

'Doctor Livingstone, I presume,' said Jane.

He stared at her dumbly. She was wearing a shaggy white bathrobe, her head bare, her feet in sandals, and his first coherent thought was that in the matter of costume she went from strength to strength, for it seemed to him that, though it was a near thing, she presented an even more enchanting spectacle thus than in the more conventional costume in which he had seen her on previous occasions. Swallowing in order to restore to its base the heart which appeared to have leaped into his mouth, he said.

'You startled me!'

'I thought I noticed you jump. Guilty conscience. You're trespassing.'

'I suppose I am.'

'Never mind. I won't hand you over to the police.'

'Algy told me to meet him here.'

'Then while you're waiting for him we can talk, and you can tell me all about everything you have been doing since we last met.'

She dropped to the grass like a white moth settling on a leaf. A little breeze had sprung up, ruffling the surface of the lake and playing a soft tune in the rushes at the water side. It died away and the world was still again.

'Well, from the fact that you're here,' said Jane, 'I deduce that you've seen the house. What did you think of it?'

'It's peculiar.'

'I thought that would be your verdict. But this is lovely, don't you think?'

'Beautiful.'

'It ought to be. The Beau spent a fortune on it.'

'The Beau?'

'Regency buck. Flourished late seventies and early eighteen hundreds. They called him Beau Paradene, and I've often wondered why. The standard of masculine comeliness must have been very low in those days, because there's a portrait of him in the picture gallery, and he looks like Nero Wolfe.'

'Stout?'

'Bulging. I'm surprised he ever got any girl to marry him.'

Bill felt the conversation had begun to take the right turn.

'He was married, was he?'

'Yes, and from all accounts he treated her abominably. Regency husbands were like that. He used to go off and play cards all night, and when he was at home he was always drunk. He was one of the three-bottle men you read about. And just to round the thing off he was steadfastly unfaithful to her.'

Bill was horrified. She had touched on a subject on which he held the strongest views.

'A man who treats his wife like that ought to be shot!'

'I believe he was – in duels – more than once.'

'I can't imagine anyone treating his wife like that.'

'You wouldn't?'

'I certainly wouldn't.'

'No, I don't think you would.'

'I'd feel that it was my job in life to do everything to make her happy.'

'Bring her breakfast in bed?'

'Of course.'

'Dry the dishes?'

'Naturally.'

'And smoke to her when she had a headache? I think you're going to be the ideal husband when you get around to it. Somebody like you is just what the late Mrs Beau Paradene could have done with.'

A sudden dryness seemed to be paralysing Bill's vocal cords. He was feeling as Wendell Stickney had felt on a memorable occasion, that his spine was being used as an exercise ground by a considerable number of spiders. He was a humble man, and the idea of asking a girl to marry him seemed too bizarre to be entertained.

Then a healing thought occurred to him. L. P. Green had done it. So had the proprietor of the Muldoon place and Clarence Binstead, the two last-named on several occasions, showing that it could be done. Nevertheless, he still hesitated. It was all very well for James Graham, Marquis of Montrose, to speak scornfully of the man who either fears his fate too much or his deserts are small, that puts it not unto the touch, to win or lose it all, but that was precisely the position in which he found himself. Small was the exact description of his deserts, and as for fearing his fate too much, that almost understated it. What would become of him if he put it unto the touch and she said 'No' or merely told him that there were other applicants ahead of him and he would have to take his place in the queue?

Jane was regarding him tenderly. Experience enabled her to divine what was passing in his mind. Several men had proposed marriage to her in the past few years – Lionel Green in the patronizing manner of one conferring a favour, the others with just this same agitated approach, and with these last she had had no difficulty in gently expressing her regrets that she was unable to reciprocate their feelings. But this was different. This was Bill, and it had needed only Algy's revelation in the station taxi to tell her that with Bill she had reached journey's end. She had the issue perfectly straight in her mind. Bill wanted her, she wanted Bill. It was as simple as that.

Bill, wrestling with himself in silence, had overcome his craven fears. James Graham, Marquis of Montrose, would have been proud of him. Stiffening the sinews and summoning up the blood, as recommended by Shakespeare, he contrived to say in a husky voice:

'Jane.'

'Yes?'

'Jane.'

'Yes.'

'Jane.'

She came to his assistance, as a woman should.

'Shall I do it for you, Bill? Is what you are trying to say that you love me?'

Bill gulped.

'Yes.'

'And want me to marry you?'

'Yes, and I know what you are going to say, that you hardly know me and think I've got the nerve of an Army mule expecting you to so much as consider for a moment marrying an ugly devil like me whom you've only met a couple of times.'

'Four.'

'Eh?'

'Counting now. But go on.'

'It isn't as though I had anything to recommend me.'

'Haven't you?'

'Except that I loved you the first time I saw you.'

'I've nothing against love at first sight.'

'And I'll tell you something. Two days ago I wouldn't have had the gall to ask you to marry me. I hadn't anything to offer you. But I've just had a letter from that New York literary agent I told you about. He's got a publisher to publish *Deadly Ernest*.'

'How wonderful!'

'And, more than that, he's sold it to a magazine as a one-shotter for four thousand dollars.'

'That's stupendous.'

'And he says that if I come to New York and study the American market and meet the right people, he can guarantee that I'll make a packet.'

'Why, Bill, this is super-colossal.'

'I ought to get over there as soon as possible, so, Jane, Jane darling –'

'Will I marry you and come with you? Would buy me with your gold, would you? Well,' said Jane, 'it's an idea and quite a good one. Let's discuss it.'

5

When Algy arrived at the lake, the first thing he saw was his sister disporting herself in the waters, and the first thought that occurred to him was that here was an admirable opportunity of employing on Bill's behalf the eloquence of which he was always so full. It seemed to him that it would be needed, for it had not escaped his notice that Bill was nowhere to be seen, and he found the fact ominous. With so excellent a chance of pressing his suit in the most ideal surroundings, there could be no explanation of his absence other than that the squirt had handed him the pink slip, causing him to withdraw from her presence with bowed head and aching heart, a state of affairs which no brother could permit. We can't have this sort of thing going on, he was feeling as he joined Jane in mid-lake. He addressed himself to the congenial task of telling her what a decent man thought of her behaviour.

'Where's Bill?' he asked, treading water.

'He's gone,' said Jane, also treading water.

'Did you send him away?'

'No, he just went.'

'Did he press his suit?'

'Yes, I remember him doing that.'

Algy snorted bitterly. It was as he had supposed.

'Then I see what happened. I see it clearly. He laid his heart at your feet and you coldly and callously booted it over the horizon. Did it occur to you to ask him what he was doing here? I'll bet it didn't, and I shall now proceed to tell you. He came here for love of you, even though this involved passing himself off as a broker's man.'

'What!'

'But he did not hesitate. He marched right in, representing Duff and Trotter, purveyors of fine wines, spirits and liqueurs, and served the papers on Henry.'

'Oh, poor Henry!'

'Not so much of the poor Henry. It's poor Bill I'm talking about. Yes, he assumed the guise of a ruddy bailiff purely in order to get together with you. And what ensues? Were you touched? Did your heart melt? Not by a jugful. You gave him the sleeve across the windpipe and kicked him out. A splendid fellow like Bill. A chap who saved my life once.'

'He did? You never told me. When was that?'

'When we were at school. It was nearing the end of term and money was extraordinarily tight. I was down to bedrock, couldn't afford the meanest jam sandwich at the school shop. And just as I was fainting from malnutrition good old Bill suddenly produces a tin of the finest mixed biscuits sent to him by an aunt of his, and we shared them fifty-fifty. Just when the pangs of hunger had become almost insupportable. That's what I mean when I say he saved my life.'

The moral of his story was not lost on Jane.

'Most boys would have kept those biscuits for themselves, but not Bill. It was just like him to share them with you. For-bidding exterior, but heart of gold, that's Bill.'

Algy was not to be mollified.

'Forbidding exterior be blowed. You aren't so hot yourself, young Jane. Well, if you think his heart's so golden, why have you cast him aside like a –'

'Worn out glove?'

'I was going to say old tube of toothpaste. Let me tell you that if you were in France, you wouldn't be allowed to pick and choose like this when it came to marrying. Your mate would be chosen by the head of the family, and if he caught you turning down his selection, you'd be sent to bed without your supper. And that's how things ought to be run over here. I'm the head of our branch of the family, and if we were French, I'd say "Marry Bill, you fat-headed little pipsqueak" and you'd jump to it and that would be that. Why the devil don't you marry him?'

'Give us time, head of the family, give us time. We're work-ing up to it by degrees. Just before you arrived, for instance, we took a long step in the right direction by plighting our troth. You can't expect more than that in a single afternoon.'

Algy gasped.

'You and Bill are engaged?'

'We are.'

'You didn't give him the bum's rush?'

'I didn't.'

'Your answer to his proposal was in the affirmative?'

'Very much so. Enthusiastic is the word.'

Algy was justifiably indignant.

'And having this vital piece of information in your kick you kept it under your hat and allowed me to waste all that eloquence on you. Do you realize that I might quite easily have got clergyman's sore throat?'

'Still, it was great fun, wasn't it?' said Jane, and reaching out a hand she thrust him firmly into the depths.

He rose to the surface, spluttering, and for a moment remained spitting out water and regarding his sister with a jaundiced eye as she disappeared.

'Women!' he said, and not even the philosopher Schopenhauer could have spoken the word with greater bitterness.

Then kindlier thoughts prevailed. The world, he felt, was not such a bad place after all. True, it contained pipsqueaks who treated their brothers with sickening disrespect, but it also contained Splendid men, quick on the draw with their chequebooks, like Wendell Stickney. It all sort of evened up, thought Algy, it all sort of evened up.

He detached a water beetle from his hair and swam ashore.

MORE ABOUT PENGUINS, PELICANS, PEREGRINES AND PUFFINS